Spirits of the Alamo

A History of the Mission and its Hauntings

Robert Wlodarski

and

Anne Powell Wlodarski

Dedicated to those brave souls who lived, fought, and died for the cause of Texas freedom and to some who still remain, suspended in time. . . .

The Spirit of the Alamo Lives On!

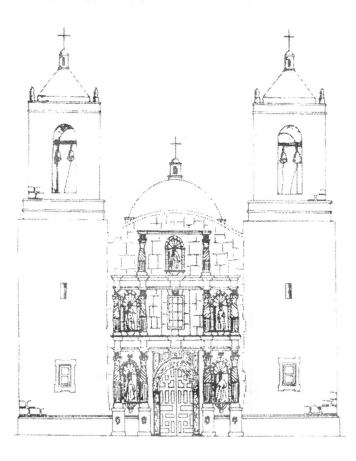

Spirits of the Alamo

A History of the Mission and its Hauntings

Robert Wlodarski

and

Anne Powell Wlodarski

Republic of Texas Press

Library of Congress Cataloging-in-Publication Data
Wlodarski, Robert James.
   Spirits of the Alamo: a history of the mission and its hauntings / Robert
   Wlodarski and Anne Powell Wlodarski.
       p.   cm.
   Includes bibliographical references and index.
   ISBN 1-55622-681-0 (pbk.)
       1. Alamo (San Antonio, Tex.)--History.   2. Ghosts--Texas--San Antonio--
   Anecdotes.   3. Alamo (San Antonio, Tex.)--Siege, 1836.   4. San
   Antonio (Tex.)--History.   I. Wlodarski, Anne Powell.   II. Title.
   F394.S28A488   1999
   976.4'351--dc21   99-10641
                                                                        CIP

2320 Los Rios Boulevard
Plano, Texas 75074

Printed in the United States of America

ISBN 1-55622-681-0
10 9 8 7 6 5 4 3 2
9901

The stories appearing in this book are based on factual accounts of
everyday people who have either visited or been employed at the Alamo.
Some stories have originally appeared in somewhat different form in the
book *Spirits of San Antonio and South Texas* (1993) by Docia Schultz
Williams and Reneta Byrne.

All photographs and illustrations are provided courtesy of The Institute of
Texan Cultures; the Center for Archaeological Research, The University of
Texas at San Antonio; or the Daughters of the Republic of Texas unless
otherwise noted. The contents of this book do not reflect the opinions of
the Daughters of the Republic of Texas.

All inquiries for volume purchases of this book should be addressed to
Wordware Publishing, Inc., at the above address. Telephone inquiries may
be made by calling:

(972) 423-0090

Contents

Acknowledgements

We would like to thank the following individuals: Ginnie Bivona and the fine staff at Wordware Publishing for carefully revitalizing the original *Haunted Alamo* book and producing this updated version; former Alamo employee Brenda Gragg; Anne Fox at the Center for Archaeological Research, The University of Texas at San Antonio; Waynne Cox of PASTQUEST Archaeological Consulting for an enlightening tour of the Alamo and providing his expertise in reviewing the historical accuracy of our book; Diane Bruce of The University of Texas at San Antonio, Institute of Texan Cultures, for her help in obtaining historical photographs of the Alamo without which the text would not have come to life; Kathleen Bittner, renowned psychic, who walked through the Alamo with us and provided her impressions of the spirited grounds; Hector Venegas of the historic and ghostly Menger Hotel and Peter Ells of the equally impressive and equally haunted Crown Plaza St. Anthony Hotel for providing lodging while we conducted our Alamo interviews; Susan Yerkes of the *San Antonio Express* for her newspaper articles, which aided us in our quest for stories; *FATE Magazine* for placing a request in Report from the Readers, which triggered a wonderful response; Cathy Herpich, Library Director for The Daughters of the Republic of Texas Library; Russell Stultz of Wordware Publishing, Inc., Plano, Texas, for granting us permission to excerpt material from *Spirits of San Antonio and South Texas*, a wonderful book by Docia Schultz Williams and Reneta Byrne; The Library of Congress for providing copies of the Historical American Buildings Survey (HABS), architectural drawings, and historical information pertaining to Mission San Antonio de Valero; Somerset chief of police Robert L. Dean, Monte Lee, William MacKeen, and a cadre of former Alamo rangers who came forward with stories about their encounters while working at the Alamo; Dee Gurnett, who helped locate those willing to talk to us, and those kindred spirits of the Alamo Society, who provided assistance along the way; the Alamo rangers, who have patrolled the grounds dutifully for years. Some have seen the spirits pass before their dubious eyes and came forward to speak for the first time while others have seen but remain silent; and last, but certainly not least, Martin Leal, who conducts the Hauntings History of San Antonio every day of the year (210-436-5417).

Preface

That ghosts exist is difficult to dispute, for they have long since been an integral part of the world of the living, both philosophically, spiritually, and psychologically; however, there are still those who choose to ignore the centuries of evidence, their own intuition and feelings, and, instead, are waiting for science to provide conclusive evidence for survival after death. What many know in their heart, that the dead return and angels exist, others reject because they have not seen with their own eyes that otherworldly phenomena occur. The fact is, even if they saw a ghost or apparition, they would still probably deny what they saw, attributing the event to some scientific explanation. It is their loss not to be open to such possibilities, such thoughts and feelings which bind us to the unseeable, to an energy that is timeless, to a belief that the spirit survives death, and immortality is possible.

The stories that have been gathered from most cultures over thousands of years attest to either a type of cross-cultural psychologically induced phenomena or "something" that we cannot easily explain away, which exists just beyond our normal sensory experience, an intangible energy called ghosts or spirits. Ghosts emerge from ordinary conditions related to everyday circumstances, death due to natural causes, as well as extraordinary circumstances, which derived from extreme emotional crises, murder, suicide, accidents, or war; however, the questions of why and how ghosts exist within the framework of the paranormal still remain a topic of hot debate awaiting final resolution.

If one were to go back to the beginning of man's existence on this planet with the belief that ghosts exist and assume that every person who has ever died represents a potential haunting, virtually every spot on earth would contain some form of psychic imprint or residual energy, essentially making this a haunted world. What if every death leaves a psychic imprint and the dead are continually walking or floating side-by-side with the living, but our senses are not attuned to their vibration? Or, perhaps all of us have the psychic gift but few use it, and those who do see with a different sensory vision.

One thing is certain: To judge paranormal phenomena in human terms seems a disservice to their remnant energy and suggests that we may be limited in our perception of things we cannot control or understand. Therefore, this book follows a long line of others in doing what those interested in this subject matter do best: that is, to faithfully document the subject matter of ghosts as factually as possible and, like a good historian, provide the data and leave the judging to others.

The authors are believers because we have been fortunate enough to touch "the other side," to have experienced the possibility of an afterlife, something beyond our mortality. It is a little frightening to hear or see something that, by basic sensory experience, should not be there, but it is also exhilarating to be "touched" by something beyond our limited senses and, for a brief moment, realize that our spirit, or god-like energy, survives death. We believe that we are not alone here, that other dimensions or levels of energy co-exist alongside us, waiting for the moment when we are able to remove our blinders and use our psychic abilities to truly see all of the wonderful things which lie just beyond our normal field of vision.

Introduction

Welcome to the Alamo, a place that conjures up nostalgic feelings and where, with a little imagination, one can almost feel the energy rising from these hallowed grounds. The Alamo is best known for a battle between Texans and Mexican forces that would forever change the face of the West. The Alamo lies between Alamo Plaza, East Crockett, East Houston, and Bonham Streets. This area represents a focal point in the early history of San Antonio before a Lone Star State was even conceived.

After visiting the heart of San Antonio and reviewing the history of the Alamo, it is easy to understand why ghosts or spirits may frequent the hallowed grounds of this very special place. The Alamo attained mythical status after the famous battle fought on March 6, 1836, and continues to draw people from all over the world. Even though the edifice, a testament to those on both sides who gave their lives for a noble cause, has been modified and lies in cramped quarters surrounded by other historical structures, it still represents a lasting tribute to the spirit of San Antonio.

The Alamo history includes legends, heroes, martyrs, and ghosts. The Alamo is the most popular tourist attraction in Texas and will probably always be close to everyone's heart. With such a legacy, how could it not be?

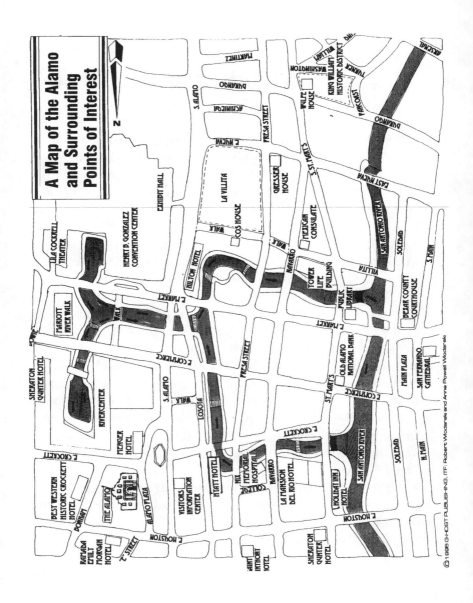

A Map of the Alamo and Surrounding Points of Interest

The Alamo: To Honor the Dead

In San Antonio and parts of South Texas, things occasionally do go bump in the night. While San Antonio may be the number-one tourist destination in Texas, it may also be one of the most haunted cities in the entire state. Steeped in history and tradition, San Antonio has numerous buildings and locations that many claim are also home for some interesting and intriguing spirits.

Docia Schultz Williams and Reneta Byrne,
Spirits of San Antonio and South Texas (1993)

Every story dealing with ghosts and the paranormal has a basis in history that provides a reference point for the haunting. It may be the location of an Indian burial ground now under a housing tract, a Civil War battlefield, or a particular battle in a war. It can be a general or specific point in time and space that relates to an event which appears to leave an indelible imprint on our landscape. Sometimes the energy of a particular person or group of people dissipates after an event. Other times, the remnant energy leaves an imprint or scar as if the event becomes frozen in time, repeating or reappearing again and again. It can be an image, a smell, a feeling, a sound, or some residual psychic sensory energy that is left over and picked up by one of our senses.

1

Drawing of the Alamo in 1838 by Mary A. Maverick
From Hard (Ed.), A Historical Overview of Alamo Plaza and Camposanto, (1994:47)

To a ghost, 500 years might very well be five seconds. Perhaps time simply stands still for the dead while generations of the living continue to record the events or pass them down orally as legends and lore. That is how ghost stories become a part of our history, a chronicle of events that we may possibly add to one day; who knows! With this in mind, the ghost stories of the Alamo unfold within a very special historic context, one that many boldly called the cradle of Texas liberty.

Native Americans and the Spanish

The history of the Alamo has been long and involved, spanning more than 250 years, and it has shaped the lives of many peoples with differing ethnic and cultural backgrounds through a series of turbulent historical events. The Alamo Shrine, originally a mission church, dates from 1744 when the cornerstone was laid, but it is the end product of earlier developments which began in 1700 in what is now the State of Coahuila in northeastern Mexico.

Jack Eaton, *Excavations at the Alamo Shrine* (1980)

Much of the following historical information contained herein was excerpted from Myers (1948), T.R. Fehrenbach (1968), Nevin (1975), Fox et al. (1976), Eaton (1980), Fox (1992), and Hard (ed. 1994). The history of what is now called San Antonio dates back well beyond the Spanish, Mexican, and Texan era. It is rooted in Native American culture, that of the Tonkawa and their ancestors who hunted and gathered in the Edwards Plateau Region, portions of the coastal plains to the south, and in the Brazos River drainage to the east. The Tonkawa were considered part of the Plains Indian culture and became organized into a tribal group during the 1600s and 1700s.

Spanish interest in an area that would later be called Texas began on a passive note when Spanish explorer Alvarez de Piñeda sailed along the Gulf Coast from Florida to Tampico in 1519. Spain had little interest in the area for over 150 years until Frenchman Sieur de La Salle accidentally landed along the Texas coastline in 1689. With La Salle, the door opened for European interests, and conflict with existing Native American cultures began. La Salle opened Spain's eyes to the New World, one which they believed they controlled. Fear of French intrusion prompted a response by Spain in 1689. Spain sent De Leon to the frontier lands accompanied by Franciscan friars Damian Massanet and Francisco Hidalgo. Both were trained for frontier life at the Franciscan Apostolic College of Santa Cruz de Queretaro.

Three expeditions followed De Leon, culminating in the establishment of Mission San Francisco de los Tejas at the remains of the destroyed French Fort Saint Louis in 1690 followed by missions on the Red, Neches, and Guadalupe Rivers by 1691. During the late 1690s the Spanish first camped along a river they named San Antonio de Padua. This attempt at colonizing the territory for Spain lasted only a few years. By 1693 attacks by Native Americans, food shortages, and the death of their cattle proved too much for the King of Spain, who viewed this as a project in which costs greatly exceeded productivity. Hence, the mission frontier concept was abandoned. By the late 1600s Native American groups of southern Texas were facing a decline in population and the loss of their homeland. Disease decimated much of their population, and assimilation into European culture greatly compromised their ethnic identity.

In 1699, after an unsuccessful attempt by the Franciscans to operate their newly founded mission, San Juan Bautista, on the Rio de Sabinas north of Monclova, Mexico, friars Antonio de San Buenaventura y Olivares, Marcos de Guerena, and Francisco Hidalgo relocated their missions further to the north in the Valle de la Circumcision near freshwater springs—roughly two leagues from the Rio Grande where the present town of Guerrero in the state of Coahuila now stands. The relocated mission was founded on January 1, 1700. Shortly after its founding, the military, under the command of Sergeant Major Diego Ramon, arrived to provide protection. A presidio was constructed near the mission, which would become the heart of Spanish colonization efforts in the region. The founding of Mission San Bernardo in 1702 under the direction of Father Alonso Gonzalez, the third mission located near an important crossing along the Rio Grande, formed what was known as the gateway to Spanish Texas—an area that witnessed the beginning of most explorations and military campaigns into the frontier province of Texas. Problems with Mission San Francisco Solano led Fathers Antonio and Hidalgo to relocate the mission to the west of the original, renaming it Mission San Ildefonso, located near the present town of Zaragoza, Mexico. Continued attacks by the Native American populations forced the abandonment of many missions—San Ildefonso being no exception. This mission was moved again in 1712 and acquired a new name: Mission San José.

By 1714 Spain's lack of concerted effort to protect its frontier resulted in an intrusion by a French trading expedition under Louis Juchereau de St. Denis, who entered East Texas, reaching the presidio at San Juan Bautista on the Rio Grande. In 1717 Spain decided it was time to secure the frontier once and for all. It initiated a plan to establish a series of missions that could depend upon one another for support in a kind of mission "network system," a system which was lacking in earlier attempts to colonize the land and contributed to its abandonment. A new mission was proposed that would bridge the gap between the Rio Grande and East Texas, the location of the site being along the San Antonio River. It was determined that the staff for the new mission would come from San José on the Rio Grande, a mission that was constantly having problems. Eventually, six missions were established by the early 1700s within what is now the city of San

5

Antonio (the only city in the United States to have that many missions within its city limits).

Mission San José lasted until 1718 when it was again moved north into Texas to a more desirable spot along the Camino Real between the Rio Grande and the missions in east Texas, preferably along the Rio San Antonio at a place called "Yanaguana" by the Native Americans. This had been the dream of Fathers Massanet and Hidalgo ever since they briefly visited the area in 1691 as part of a military expedition. They commented on the beauty of the area as well as the abundance of potential converts. On April 9, 1718, Father Olivares; his assistant, Father Mezquia; Martin de Alarcon, governor of Coahuila y Tejas (Texas); and seven families crossed the Rio Grande on their way to establish a new settlement in East Texas—a settlement which would not only serve to convert the local Native Americans but also as a supply point for other missions in the region. Sixteen days later the group reached a verdant valley fed by the San Antonio River.

Setting off on their own, Olivares and Mezquia located a suitable spot for the new mission on the west bank of the San Antonio River near San Pedro Springs (in an area now known as Brackenridge Park). On May 5 they named the mission San Antonio de Valero in honor of Saint Anthony de Padua and the Viceroy of Spain, Marquis de Valero. At the same time, Governor Alarcon formally established the Villa de Bejar (later changed to Bexar), a civil and military outpost, in honor of the brother of the Viceroy of Spain, not far from the intended location of the mission. In less than a year, the site of the mission was relocated to the east side of the river. The actual construction of the present church was not begun for many years. In the meantime, the necessity for supplying water to the location took precedence.

Construction on an acequia (irrigation ditch) began in 1719 to provide water to the fledgling mission, tapping the San Antonio River south of its headwaters at present-day Brackenridge Park. Attacks by local Native Americans and a devastating hurricane in 1724 once again required the relocation of the mission. In 1727 Father Miguel Sevillana de Paredes inspected the mission and noted that a small fortification was in existence (less than 300 meters from its present location). By now, Olivares and Mesquia were replaced by Father Hidalgo and his assistant, Father José Gonzalez. The attacks by Apaches made construction of both the acequia and a permanent mission a slow process with only a temporary church, convent rooms, and a granary in use by a population of 70 families (280 people) by 1727, representing three nations: the Xarames, the Payayas, and the Yerebipiamos (Barker 1929).

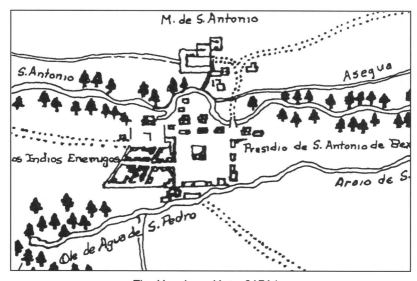

The Menchaca Map of 1764
From Fox et. al., The Archaeology and History of Alamo Plaza (1976:13)

By 1730 the residents of the mission had replaced the temporary church with a flat-roofed interim structure located immediately to the south of the convento facing toward the west. This structure would be replaced by a permanent building awaiting the hewn stone and craftsmen to complete the job. Founded as the first civil settlement of Spanish Texas in 1731, the plan for the presidio of San Antonio de Bexar followed earlier Spanish efforts at settlement, which were confined to the establishment of a series of mission and military outposts in the eastern and southern parts of the province. In order to consolidate the settlement of this portion of Texas as well as solving the problem of supplying food to the presidio, the viceroy resolved to create Bexar.

Permission to settle was also accompanied by detailed instructions on how to proceed with one of the earliest examples of urban planning in the American western frontier—the same plan used in Santa Fe, New Mexico. Although the arrangement of the streets surrounding the main plaza varied somewhat from the laws of the Indies planning pattern, the Plano de la Poblacion of San Antonio de Bexar was implemented and otherwise generally conformed with Spanish specifications, which included a requirement for the orientation of the grid street system in order that the four corners of the plaza and of the street blocks face the cardinal directions of the compass.

A change in the planning concept for Bexar occurred when the site described in the instructions sent with Alarcon proved unsatisfactory. Instead, the town was founded immediately adjacent to the military post, altering the prescribed plan by reducing the size of the main plaza and shifting the street grid by forty-five degrees. Therefore, the streets and plaza of colonial San Antonio provided the basic structure for the town as it grew and expanded over the next 100 years. The plaza and church served as their focus for social and religious life with its one-story adobe buildings surrounding the plaza and enclosing it in almost the exact manner it had been envisioned by Spanish officials.

In 1739 an epidemic (probably smallpox) reduced the mission to roughly 46 families, or 184 individuals. Within a year 76 new converts of Tamiques Indians increased the diminished population. Father Benito Fernandez de Santa Ana, the head of all the missions in Villa de Bexar, claimed that mission San Antonio de Valero could withstand a siege better than any other presidio in the province. By 1745 Father Francisco Xavier Ortiz had succeeded Father Hidalgo and was finally able to report that construction of the permanent church made of cut stone and lime mortar was underway. Actually, the construction had begun on May 8, 1744, with the laying of the cornerstone of the church. In the meantime, services were still conducted within the confines of the interim structure, which now administered to a population of 311.

The missionaries occupied a small, two-story friary, constructed of stone and mortar, with three rooms on the second story for living and multipurpose rooms on the first floor. Adjacent to the living quarters was a large gallery where the Indian women made clothing, followed by a granary, and finally a series of rooms that were used by officers. Meanwhile, the mission Indians lived in two rows of small adobe huts made of straw-thatched roofs, which lined the acequia and coursed through the plaza. Along each row of huts was a dirt street surrounded in its entirety by an adobe wall.

Father Ortiz returned in 1756 and remarked on the slow progress of church construction. He noted that it had to be demolished due to a poor foundation and reconstructed. The reconstructed church fared no better as Father Mariano Francisco de los Dolores reported in 1762

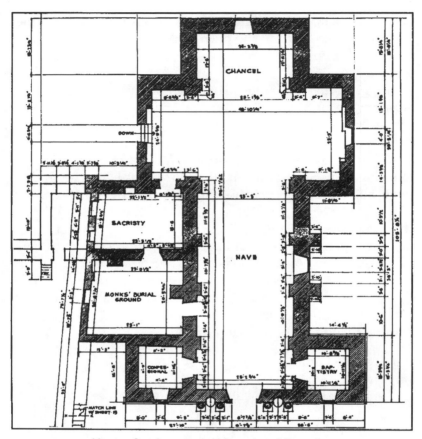

Mission San Antonio de Valero chapel floor plan
Historic American Buildings Survey (TEX-318)

that the reconstructed church had collapsed due to "poor expertise." He also noted that the sacristy was still incomplete. The housing of the neophytes had increased to seven rows of stone huts to form a plaza, which the acequia, now lined with willow and fruit trees, passed through. A tower was constructed at the gate in the south wall to assist in the defense of the mission. The population now included 76 families with 275 men, women, and children. In

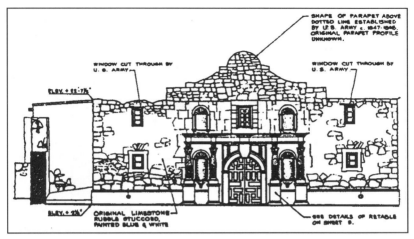

Mission San Antonio de Valero west elevation plan
Historic American Buildings Survey (TEX-318)

addition, 1,972 baptisms had been performed, 454 marriages recorded, and 1,247 people buried. The mission pueblo consisted of thirty adobe houses, twenty with doors and arches. There were also other structures of a less permanent nature.

In 1772 the Franciscan college of Nuestra Senora de Guadalupe de Zacatecas took control of the Spanish missions in Mexico y Coahuilla whereby the transfer of administrative duties resulted in an inventory of each mission. Mission San Antonio de Valero was described as being made up of five rows of houses, each row having three houses, and each house being eight varas long with a door to the east and a window to the west. The houses had corridors or porches of stone arches for lighting and for the convenience of those who lived there. Two other houses were located outside of those mentioned, without porches, but were well built to protect against rain and wind.

11

In 1789 Father José Lopez, the head of the missions in the region, mentioned that Mission San Antonio de Valero was almost built in the shape of a square and was surrounded by a stone and mud wall that stood roughly 300 paces from the center. The same rampart served as a wall for a majority of the fifteen or sixteen houses, while providing ample lodging for the Indians. Nearly all houses were covered with wood and mortar as a protection against the rain and had hand-carved, wooden doors with locks and iron keys. A granary of stone and lime was located within the square with a house adequate for the missionaries and officers located adjacent to it. The structures were built of stone and lime with good roofs, doors, windows, and locks.

Lopez also noted that a sacristy (which today, serves as the church while another room serves as the sacristy) adjoined the officers' quarters. Both structures were constructed of stone and mortar with arched roofs. The church, under construction, contained a very large nave whose walls were built as high as the cornices with the latter having been built only in the dome of the presbytery. In the front, its beautiful facade of wrought stone was not completed to the same height as the walls (the church, however, was never completed due to lack of qualified workmen). The chapel, part of the mission complex, ceased to be operational in 1793 due to the secularization of the mission. According to Fox, et al. (1976:5), at the time of secularization, the mission was enclosed by a rectangular wall approximately 8.3 feet high made of both stone and adobe. The north wall was already in ruin. The buildings were stripped of their valuables, including the locks and doors, and were unoccupied for almost a decade.

All the while, the local Native American tribes continued to harass the missionaries, their converts, and the military forces stationed there. A nine-year hiatus in the occupation of the mission, combined with Spain's fear that France or the United States might attempt to settle the Texas frontier, resulted in Spain sending a company of soldiers to the Presidio of Bexar to augment a small detachment that was stationed there in December 1802. It was the arrival of the Compania Volante de San Carlos de San José y Santiago de Parras del Alamo under the command of Colonel Anastasio Bustamente to the "Presidio de Bexar" that gave rise to the change of the mission name from San Antonio de Valero to simply "the Alamo." Establishing its troops in the old mission, the "Flying Company" erected barracks along the south compound wall and inside the abandoned buildings.

Anastasio Bustamante opened a hospital in a deserted mission building and equipped it with reed beds, a male nurse, and a female cook in 1805. In 1806 two rooms were added in the abandoned mission as a pharmacy. All the while, the church continued to serve the religious needs of the small community of neophytes, soldiers, and their families. In 1809 additional repairs were reported, and in 1810 they were carried out. This included a new roof and gutter, repair of the floors, and repair of the damaged walls with small rocks and mortar.

From 1805 to 1810 the seeds of revolution were festering in New Spain, both from within and without its borders. On January 6, 1809, reports that 4,000 United States troops were being sent to New Orleans, with an additional 50,000 under the command of General James Wilkinson to be stationed at the Texas-Louisiana border, began circulating to Manuel Salcedo (the acting governor of Texas) from his uncle, Nemecio Salcedo (the Commandant General of the Northeast Provinces of New Spain). The younger Salcedo, taking the information as a warning, began fortifying the Alamo, which would serve as a primary stronghold should there be an invasion by foreigners.

While the army of New Spain was preparing for an invasion from the United States, their true enemy came from within. Father Miguel Hidalgo y Costilla, with a ragtag army of Indians, Mestizos, and Creoles, declared their independence from Spain in the village of Dolores. By 1811 the insurgency had spread to San Antonio de Bexar. Fueled by fear and anxiety, rumors spread that the Spanish garrison stationed there was going to abandon Bexar and leave a defenseless population exposed to the rebels. On the evening of January 21, 1811, retired Spanish Captain Juan Bautista Casas established his headquarters in the Alamo, and the revolution reached the frontier.

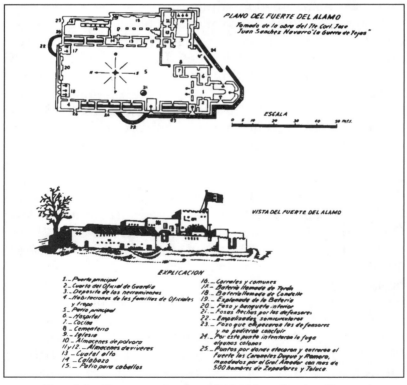

Plan of the Alamo complex drawn by José Juan Sanchez Navarro
Courtesy of The Institute of Texan Cultures, San Antonio

14

However, within six months the revolution was suppressed, and both the treasonous Casas and Hidalgo paid with their lives. The growing unrest within the heart of Mexico required that all outpost garrisons be recalled to protect the threatened government. After almost ten years of occupying the presidio and church, the Alamo garrison left on April 1, 1812, after relinquishing its records to the parish church. Spain's control in New Spain was on the verge of extinction. Hidalgo's dream of freedom did not end with his death at the hands of the Spanish, nor did his death dampen the revolutionary zeal of others committed to the task of ending the reign of Spain in the Americas. With Hidalgo's defeat, the Louisiana-Texas border now became a hotbed. On August 10, 1812, José Bernardo Maximiliano Gutierrez de Lara united with William Augustus Magee and crossed the Sabine River with a small force of 130 men, taking Nacogdoches. After a series of successful skirmishes with Spanish troops along the way, the small army occupied La Bahia in November.

Samuel Kemper assumed control of Magee's force when he died in February 1813. Kemper moved 800 men from a besieged La Bahia in March and headed for Bexar. He and his men seized the town and a small band of loyalist officers under the leadership of Spanish Governor Manuel Salcedo on April 2, 1813. The insurgent force occupied the Alamo after executing Salcedo and his officers. The Alamo by this time was in a sad state and badly in need of repairs. However, even a concerted effort by those remaining in Bexar could do little to help the Alamo with a facelift.

Meanwhile, the Spanish were mounting an offensive to quell this rebellion. Under General Joaquin de Arredondo, his army of 4,000 marched toward Bexar to put an end to the rebels. The insurgents were no match for Arredondo's army. On the battlefield south of the Medina River, 600 of Kemper's men were killed, and 327 more men were

15

executed in Bexar. The immediate effect of this carnage was to demoralize the revolutionary movement in the region as well as depopulating it of potential malcontents.

Mexicans and Texians

A man who has nothing which he cares about more than his personal safety, is a miserable creature who has no chance of being free, unless made and kept so by the exertions of better men than himself.

John Stuart Mill

In 1821, after years of dreaming and fighting for freedom, Mexico finally forced the Spanish out of the Americas. Vicente Iturbide became emperor, and temporary stability was established in Mexico. Iturbide, wishing to improve conditions on the frontier, sent troops under Colonel Domingo de Ugartechea to Villa de Bexar, which was only a shadow of its former self after the battle of Medina. With the arrival of the troops, the population, feeling a renewed sense of protection and safety, grew to approximately 5,000. Even with the size of the population and the presence of the military, the Comanches continued to raid Bexar and surrounding areas. In the same year, Stephen Fuller Austin was granted permission to settle into the easternmost regions of Mexico with Anglo-Americans.

The 300 families he recruited were, for the most part, common folk with the basic hope of bettering their lives in a new land, which was being given away. These pioneering families were not alone, however. With them came adventurers, soldiers, smugglers, gamblers, speculators, slave traders, debtors, pirates, and fugitives as well as doctors, lawyers, and other professionals from the United States. The lawful and the lawless worked side by side in this new land, for different reasons; and there was plenty of land for everyone—the first 300 families of Texas became the stock of Texas pride.

Initially, Austin was given full military authority over his founding colony, and he governed wisely. By 1822 his original colony had grown to more than 8,000 inhabitants, some of whom gradually became involved in the political situation, expressing their desire to become free from Mexico. Times were changing in Mexico as the liberal government was gradually giving way to a military mentality thanks to Antonio Lopez de Santa Anna Perez de Lebron. In 1824 the liberalism that helped define Mexican politics gave way to a military dictatorship when the Mexican Constitution of 1824 was abolished.

In 1825 the legislature of Coahuilla passed a new colonization law for Texas that would open up more land to Roman Catholics who could prove Christian belief, and immigration was allowed to individuals or through empresarios (there were 26 in colonial Texas). Stephen F. Austin, Green DeWitt, and Martin de Leon were the primary empresarios attempting to colonize at this time. Conflicts arose over where DeWitt and De Leon would be allowed additional land to colonize. De Leon, because of his Mexican heritage, was granted first choice of land and chose his capital at Victoria while DeWitt's people returned to Gonzales. A feud over colony land and boundaries ensued, and it took Austin to finally settle the arguments.

Another colonizer named Haden Edwards entered the scene, causing problems when he located his colony near the Sabine. Conflicting claims between Mexicans and Anglos, coupled with the desire by the Anglos to be free of the often arbitrary treatment in favor of the Mexican population, laid the groundwork for revolution. Other colonizers during this period included David Burnet, Joseph Vehlein, and Lorenzo de Zavala in Galveston Bay; Sterling Robertson, north of Austin's colony; Arthur Wavell and Benjamin

Milam deep in northeast Texas; James Power and James Hewetson between the Lavaca and Nueces Rivers; and McMullen and McGloin south of San Antonio. They came from England, Scotland, Kentucky, Tennessee, Missouri, and Arkansas and fought with the original landowners, the Choctaws and Cherokees.

Between 1823 and 1829, changes were made to the Alamo by the military. By 1829 over 300 troops were being housed in the old convento buildings, and only the church and convento were apparently church owned. In 1829 Spain made a final attempt to retake Mexico. This vain effort was repelled by Santa Anna at the battle of Tampico, propelling him into national prominence. Born in Jalapa, Vera Cruz, in 1795, to a Spanish father and Creole mother, his involvement with war began at the early age of sixteen when he entered the Royal Spanish Regiment. His love of fighting and power were only equaled by his love for women. Both passions consumed him. By 1830 the Texas territory was ruled by Anglo-hating Don Manuel Mier y Teran. Soldiers were stationed at Nacogdoches under Colonel Don José de las Piedras at Anahuac on Galveston Bay under Captain Juan Bradburn, and at Velasco at the mouth of the Rio Brazos under Colonel Don Domingo de Ugartechea. Smaller forces were stationed at the Presidio of Teran on the Neches, and at La Bahia, now called Goliad (an anagram in honor of Father Hidalgo). In addition, the troops at San Antonio de Bexar were increased.

Between 1831 and 1832 tensions between the Anglos and Mexicans in the Texas territory increased. This was primarily due to the edict of April 6, 1830, which restricted immigration into the rapidly growing borderlands. The first place to reach the boiling point was the fort at Velasco on the Rio Brazos. Here, John Austin and a small army overwhelmed Mexican Colonel Ugartechea whose garrison suffered many losses before surrendering. His remaining troops were spared and allowed to return to Mexico, a gesture that was not reciprocated by the Mexicans in later battles. Austin was headed toward Anahuac to continue his campaign when news of a truce between the Mexicans and Anglos reached him. The Anahuac campaign was over, and John Austin died a short time later. His conquest was short-lived as was his reputation. All the while, Santa Anna consolidated his power, promoting political intrigue and waiting for his moment to seize control of power in Mexico. When his predecessors Iturbide, Guerrero, and Bustamante could not provide the stability and leadership necessary to implement a democratic government, militarism, under Santa Anna, became the law of the land.

Matamoros was captured by Santa Anna's forces (called Santanistas) under Colonel José Antonio Mexia in July 1832. Hearing of the insurrection at Anahuac and determined to bring an end to the rebellion, Mexia marched toward the Brazos. Fortunately, Austin, the peacemaker, reached Mexia before he was able to confront the Anglos on the Brazos. Stephen Austin skillfully persuaded Mexia that the fighting was personal, that it was among angry men who were on edge rather than between countries. Mexia reached the Brazos and was overwhelmed by the pro-Mexican support displayed by the Anglo settlers. A major catastrophe was averted, and a content Mexia, certain that these Anglos supported Mexico and his excellency Santa Anna, returned to Mexico.

Meanwhile, Bustamante fell out of favor with those who controlled political destinies—in particular, Santa Anna. The hero of Tampico decided that a change in leadership was necessary, and he threw his support in the presidential elections to Gomez Pedraza (a tyrant he once denounced and who almost had Santa Anna killed). Santa Anna had the uncanny knack of knowing which way the wind was blowing politically, and he seemed to bend like a willow in the direction that would benefit him in the long run—one of the keys to his political longevity.

On October 1, 1832, in San Felipe, sixteen Anglo-Texan districts (minus Goliad's delegation, which arrived late) held a convention and voted Stephen Austin as its president while passing a number of resolutions for the colonies including organizing militias for defense against the Indians. Finally, they all reaffirmed their allegiance to Mexico. News of the meeting reached the governor of Coahuilla and Santa Anna. Both reacted with consternation, denouncing the convention and threatening retaliation, even though the colonists fully supported the Mexican government.

A second convention was held on April 1 in San Felipe. The difference in six months was astounding. Tolerance for Mexico and Santa Anna was wearing thin. This was evident in their new choice for president. Peacemaker Austin was replaced by William Wharton, backed by David Burnet, Sam Houston, and others who were decidedly of the mind that Texas should now be self-governed.

Within one year, Austin had gone from the president of the Anglo-Texas districts to a virtual delivery boy. He unhappily agreed to his nomination to carry the revised resolutions to the government in Mexico City. These resolutions, filled with grievances, were intended to further distance the Texas frontier from Mexico's control. The framing of the resolutions, which were also intended to be submitted to Congress, was based on a process every state that entered the Union since 1792 had followed. In essence, Austin was carrying the framework to separate Anglo Texas from Mexico.

A Prelude to War

Mexicans! Watch closely, for you know all too well the Anglo-Saxon greed for territory. We have generously granted land to these Nordics; they have made their homes with us, but their hearts are with their native land. We are continually in civil wars and revolutions; we are weak, and know it—and they know it also. They may conspire with the United States to take Texas from us. From this time, be on your guard!

From a speech to a secret session
of the Mexican Congress in 1830

Leaving Texas on April 22, Austin arrived in Mexico City after a long journey that began in early July of 1833. Mexico City was going through a cholera epidemic (as well as political turmoil). Essentially, Gomez had no real power because Santa Anna controlled the army and, therefore, the government. In 1833 Santa Anna ran for presidency with Valentin Gomez Farias, a liberal, and turned over executive power to Farias to see how liberalism would fare. This way, he could sit back and take credit if it worked or interfere if it didn't.

Within a short time it became obvious that the liberal policies Farias embraced alienated the landowners, the soldiers, and the Catholic Church. With Santa Anna absent from the capital and Farias in temporary control, Austin had a difficult time obtaining a decision regarding his territorial concerns. By late September, Austin, still estranged from his homeland in Mexico City, for the first time in his illustrious career responded to his desperate situation out of anxiety and anger rather than sound judgment. He wrote an inflammatory letter to the governor of San Antonio while he languished in a political purgatory discussing the subject of statehood for the Texas territories. This presumptuous attitude by Austin would not only anger the governor, but it would come back to haunt him—essentially reshaping the destiny of Anglo-Texans. In November 1833 Santa Anna returned to the capital and heard Austin's petitions. Summarily dismissing most of them, Santa Anna did grant some concessions, which Austin took as a positive sign of cooperation and potential agreement between Mexico and the Texas territories. At the very least, Austin considered the doors open to further negotiations, a fact that pleased him when he wrote his fellow countryman discussing Santa Anna's position.

Unbeknownst to Austin, who left the capital on December 10 ever hopeful that peace would prevail, his hastily composed letter to the governor of San Antonio reached Mexico City. While on his way home, Austin stopped in Saltillo in January 1834 and was quickly arrested by presidential decree and sent back to Mexico where he would spend the next eighteen months in total isolation in the Prison of the Inquisition. His letter was considered treasonous. It took Peter Grayson and Spencer Jack, two colonial lawyers, to secure Austin's release on bail. Strangely, during his incarceration, many of the demands made by the colonists were granted. However, events were already set in motion that would propel Mexico and the Texas colonies toward war.

First, Santa Anna took full reign of the Mexican government with Farias relegated to a minor role in April of 1834. He was now the Emperor of Mexico, the Napoleon of the West. This vocal champion of the 1824 Constitution had it abolished in October 1835, proclaiming that the Mexican people were not advanced enough to live in a democracy. The second event was the result of Austin's hatred for Mexico and Santa Anna. Finally set free though

23

never pardoned or cleared of charges, the once good-natured and receptive Austin returned to the colonies on July 13, 1835, sickly and extremely angry. He had been turned from a dove to a hawk, one with talons that would aim for the heart of Mexico and Santa Anna, both with words and actions.

The Emperor of Mexico now faced dissidence on two fronts: Zacatecas and the Texas colonies. Not a man to fear a challenge, a confident Santa Anna would not waste his energy worrying about these minor considerations; he would merely march in and crush the insolent rebels swiftly and ruthlessly, as he had learned to do while a lieutenant under Arredondo. He would leave many dead as examples for others who might consider defying him. The Zacatecans were the most immediate problem for Santa Anna. They demanded independence and refused to disband their state militia.

Santa Anna's patience wore thin, and he detailed plans for suppression which were passed to his brother-in-law, Martin Perfecto de Cos, who accompanied him to Zacatecas. In short order, Santa Anna's regular troops destroyed the rebel Zacatecan force of 5,000 and allowed his soldiers to "indulge" themselves in the spoils of victory. Santa Anna then turned his attention to the second problem area: the Anglos in Texas who were talking of independence. However, even with the brewing discontent with Mexico by the prominent men of the Anglo-Texan colonies (the war clique), a majority of settlers still expressed their loyalty to Mexico and did not want a confrontation.

Meanwhile, a bitter and disillusioned Austin and fellow hawks agreed that Santa Anna could never be dealt with in a rational manner. War seemed inevitable. The once tactful and peace-loving Austin now urged his fellow Texians to fight for his dream at all costs. He petitioned those in the United States to help in the cause of freedom.

To Austin, Mexican abuse and callousness now meant that war and a force of arms were the only recourse to defend the rights of "his" settlers. It was a very personal war to Austin, now.

After his swift victory in Zacatecas, Santa Anna sent Cos from Matamoros to take over the Alamo and protect the Mexican frontier from any transgressions by the Anglos. Cos with his two divisions of infantry, which numbered approximately 1,400, arrived in Texas to reinforce the garrisons there. After leaving a small detachment at Goliad, Cos left for San Antonio de Bexar on October 9, 1835. By the time Cos and his army arrived, Anglos in the town of Gonzales had fired the first shots of the revolution, sending the Mexican army fleeing across the Rio Brazos. Cos was coming to Bexar to break up the foreign settlements there once and for all, and news of the incident in Gonzales only intensified his anger toward the colonists. He would straighten things out with Santa Anna's blessing.

The Siege of San Antonio

Freemen of Texas—To Arms . . . To Arms!!! Now's the day, and now's the hour.

William H. Wharton's call to action at Brazoria

The Texians saw Cos and the Mexicans as invaders while the Mexicans viewed the Anglos as ingrates and undesirables who had to be forced out of Mexico. There appeared to be no middle ground for negotiations. Austin put out a general call to arms on September 19, 1835, asking for help from fellow Americans to stand up to Santa Anna and defeat him. He reasoned that with enough Tennessee and Kentucky rifles, Santa Anna could be defeated. Austin's call came as Cos was crossing the Rio Grande into Texian (another term for Anglos occupying Mexican land) territory. Arriving in Villa de Bexar, Cos immediately began fortifying positions around the plaza and diverted the western branch of the acequia to the exterior of the old Indian Quarters along the west wall. According to Samuel Maverick, one of the town's 300 inhabitants, this was the first time the Alamo had been turned into a fort. During November 1835 Cos tore down the arches of the church, making an incline to haul a cannon to the top of the church. Cos also constructed a log palisade across the open area between the southwest corner of the church and low barracks and a parapet on the deteriorating north wall to fortify the area.

Meanwhile, Sam Houston was in the midst of a continually shifting internal struggle among delegates of the Texas colonies over who would command the army of

Texas. Houston knew the situation and Santa Anna better than any of the other choices (F.W. Johnson, James Walker Fannin, and Dr. James Grant by virtue of his relationship with Edward Burleson). Houston also knew that the war could not be won in a single battle against a powerful Mexican army but rather in smaller "hit-and-run" skirmishes designed to demoralize and wear down the enemy. In the meantime, the makeshift Texas political entity endeavored to blueprint a constitution that would legally separate Texas from Mexico. A formal constitution would also serve to legitimize Texas in an effort to gain credibility and support from the rest of the world. With the future of Texas at a critical stage, Houston became commander-in-chief; however, dissension threatened to destroy any hope the Texians had before they could even fight for their freedom.

In reality, the army of the people about to fight for the freedom of a vast colonial territory consisted of a skeleton group of Texian and non-resident volunteers under Houston, Fannin, Travis, and Bowie—hardly more than a annoying gnat to Santa Anna and his thousands of professionally trained soldiers. The group of men who were about to incur the wrath of Santa Anna may not have been professional soldiers or even one hundred percent committed to the cause of independence, but once the irreversible step was taken to confront the Mexicans, the momentum driving the Anglos and Mexicans toward ultimate victory or defeat in Mexican Texas could not be stopped. A greater force appeared to be at work.

A euphoric group of Texians, under Captain Collingsworth and fresh from their Gonzales victory, took Goliad, and the lightly defended fortress fell with little resistance. A sense of invincibility bolstered the group of about 300 men under a reluctant Stephen F. Austin, who was now commander of the Texians. With spirits raised, they moved toward a confrontation with Cos and his superior forces in San Antonio. Austin firmly believed his men with their long rifles could defeat the Mexicans. Cos, a cautious man by nature, could have defeated the Texians in open combat with his professional soldiers fighting as a unit against untrained men who would most likely have fought as individuals rather than a group. But Cos chose to remain confined to the buildings in San Antonio and sought help from Ugartechea, who had already faced the Anglos at Velasco. Morale was low among the Mexican forces still in Texas, and Cos could not count on any immediate help. As Cos waited, the army of the people, an inferior force, quickly surrounded him and his troops in San Antonio.

A Mexican standoff ensued as the Texians were confused as to what to do next now that they had their enemy under siege. Austin wanted to negotiate a settlement to remove the Mexicans while others in his army were hungry for a fight. The siege lasted into November without resolution. When Austin was called away on November 25, leadership of the troops passed to Colonel Edward Burleson. The besieged Mexicans needed hay for their animals and sent fifty men out to obtain feed. They were gunned down by Burleson's sharpshooters. Still, there was no offensive. In fact, men were deserting the army of the people, and there was talk of retreating back to Gonzales. This almost became a reality on December 4, 1835. As more men deserted, they were replaced by others from Tennessee and Kentucky who were eager to fight.

At this moment, fate intervened. As the baggage wagons were readied for a retreat, Colonel Frank Johnson, a dissenter for retreat under Burleson, remarked to Ben Milam, an old empresario, that the army should make a stand. Milam apparently shouted for the men to fall in line and go after Cos. Two hundred did including Burleson,

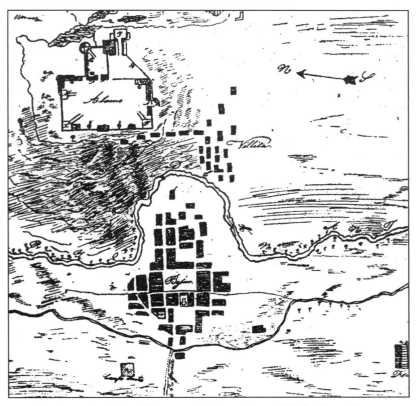

Map drawn by Colonel Ygnacio de Labastida in 1836 for Santa Anna
From Hard (Ed.), A Historical Overview of Alamo Plaza and Camposanto (1994:8)

who agreed to hold his army of 100 just outside of town while Milam's volunteers attacked. Again, Cos blundered by dividing his army between the Alamo and the town of San Antonio. Milam's assault began at 3 A.M. on December 5, and his men broke through the picket lines, quickly filing into the town. It was hand-to-hand combat, one the Anglo frontiersmen relished. The Mexican army was picked apart by the expert marksmen who were essentially snipers. Three days later, after Ben Milam had been killed during the street fighting, becoming immortalized in Texas history, Johnson became commander with Major Morris, his second in command.

Cannons and guns roared through December 8 when Cos obtained 600 reinforcements. However, his desire to fight was gone, and with the desertion of almost 200 soldiers, who fled across the Rio Grande, Cos, on December 10, 1835, surrendered with his 1,100 men at the Alamo to the army of the people, who had approximately 300 men. Burleson accepted the surrender of the Mexican army under Cos whereupon Cos signed a document in which he pledged never to fight against the colonists or against the Constitution of 1824 again. Cos took his men out of San Antonio back toward the Rio Grande. These were amazing victories for the Texians, but they created a false sense that the war was over and the Mexicans would not return. Burleson and most of the army disbanded. Still there was no centralized government, no constitution, and no plan for proceeding. Also, there were still those who opposed independence.

The Rise and Fall of the Provisonal Government

Human folly is far easier to explain than human valor.

T.R. Fehrenback, *Lone Star* (1982)

After Cos left Texas, a fundamental polarity still existed in Mexican Texas—an ethnicity gap that could not easily be bridged. The Mexican population south of the Rio Grande, both Santanistas and opponents of Santa Anna, wanted their land back from the colonists. The Anglo colonists and those who had intermarried with the Spanish and Mexicans were undecided about whether they wanted independence or to continue their allegiance to Mexico and the Mexicans or Tejanos, who were caught in no-man's-land at the time of the Independence movement. They were Mexican citizens who were distrusted by both the Anglos in Texas and the Mexicans south of the Rio Grande. Where was their true loyalty? Men like Lorenzo de Zavala, Don Juan Antonio Navarro, and Juan Nepomucena Seguin were a few of the 4,000 plus Mexican-Texans who, through their support of the Anglos, actually fought on the side of the Texians against Mexico. The others had allegiance to Mexico yet were not truly accepted by either side.

During December of 1835 the key leaders in the Texas Independence movement—Austin, Wharton, and Branch Archer—left Texas to seek help from the United States government. This was not the time to desert a fledgling freedom movement. Some felt that the more radical elements of the movement wanted any pro-Mexican sentiment out of colonial Mexico during this crucial time. This meant Austin, who still had a tendency toward conciliation and peace. Sam Houston was now named commander-in-chief of the army of Texas.

At the end of 1835, outside of a few officers who were residents of Texas, almost everyone else manning the key defensive positions at Goliad and Bexar was a volunteer who demanded action in order to continue a commitment to a cause. During this time, however, they could only wait while others decided on the next course of action. If the Mexican army came to reclaim its soil, one thing was certain; a small, paraprofessional, disorganized, and inadequately supplied army, underpaid, understaffed, and without a political portfolio, would face a superior, well-equipped, well-financed, and well-led professional army.

All that the Anglo settlers and volunteers had in their favor were a willingness to fight (if the need be), the fact that the major fortifications at Goliad and Bexar were held by the insurgents, and the 600-mile expanse of desert that was the Texas frontier and not conducive for attack by an army that had to haul all its equipment into a fight. The fact remained that the topography was the greatest weapon the Anglo settlers had because the main population centers, although part of Mexico, were not connected to it by an adequate road system. In fact, the roadways were nothing more than rutted dirt paths connecting mission-period towns, which were still being harassed by Native American tribes, the true owners of this land.

Military considerations at this time, from an Anglo settler perspective, included an attack on Matamoros. In short order, three additional commanders were appointed to lead the army of the people (Grant, Johnson, and Fannin). Houston was not even advised of the appointment. Such was the inherent chaos rampant within the so-called army ranks. Politics and the military mixed in a less-than-desirous way as no one knew who had the ultimate say in any matter, civil or military.

Colonel J.C. Neill, commanding at the Alamo, related to Governor Smith that the Matamoros expedition had seized his cannon, supplies, and clothing. The end result was that an enraged Smith chastised all involved and was subsequently relieved of his position in the council, passing control to Lieutenant Governor Robinson. Smith refused to vacate his post, and on January 17, 1836, the council, unable to raise a quorum, ceased to be. The provisional government died, and the lives of thousands of men, women, and children would be sacrificed. Without a provisional government, Sam Houston, an inspired leader, had the support of Governor Smith, Colonel Neill at San Antonio, and his recruiting officer at San Felipe, Lieutenant Colonel William Barret Travis.

The army, such as it was, without a definite military agenda and without a provisional government, still appeared to favor the taking of Matamoros, an elective proposed by the previous council. Smith dispatched Houston to Goliad to take control of the confused army and attempt to bring some semblance of order to the situation. Failing that, Smith instructed Houston to proceed into Mexico. Houston met with Grant and Johnson's force at Refugio. Meanwhile, Neill sent an urgent plea for reinforcements at the Alamo. Houston responded by sending Colonel James Bowie and a handful of men from Goliad to San Antonio to inspect the situation. He had planned to fortify Goliad and the Alamo; however, Grant and Johnson had already left San Antonio with most of the men, leaving Neill holding a tenuous position there.

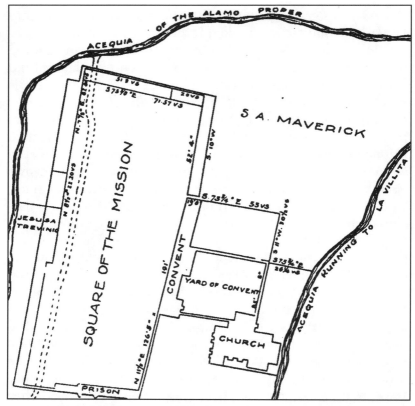

Map of the Alamo in 1849 by Francois Giraud, City Surveyor
From Hard (Ed.), A Historical Overview of Alamo Plaza and Camposanto (1994:11)

Houston wanted Bowie to assess the conditions at the Alamo and then make a decision to defend or abandon it. Although Houston probably wanted the Alamo abandoned, he did not issue an outright order to do so, leaving the decision in the hands of Bowie. Johnson, Grant, and Houston had about 500 volunteers (primarily American citizens from the south) gathered at Refugio awaiting orders. Fannin, with his 400 plus American volunteers and approximately 25 Texas volunteers, was camped near Goliad. Houston soon realized that each group of men was loyal to its own leader, and there would be no centralized or unified control of each group. They were each conducting separate operations.

Since Houston was only in charge of the "regulars," Fannin would not listen to him unless Houston agreed to place himself under the orders of the now defunct council. Four leaders would dwindle to three as Houston, viewing the strategy of the council and the other military leaders as folly, withdrew from the Matamoros expedition in order to deal with the serious Indian situation in east Texas. Fortunately, most of Grant's men followed Houston. Fannin's large force was still camped at Goliad. Travis was given orders by Governor Smith to cease recruiting efforts at San Felipe and proceed to the Alamo to help Neill. Travis took this as a sign that he would command the fort, leaving with around thirty men.

Bowie arrived at the Alamo to greet Neill and his 104 men, one cannon, and few supplies or gun powder. Not one man was a Texas settler, and nine of the contingent were ethnic Mexicans who joined the revolution. Almost every state was represented as well as men from several other countries. Essentially, where they came from was not as important as the fact they were really fontiersmen at heart. Many were hunter-trappers, doctors, and lawyers, rather than farmers. Shortly after Bowie's entrance into San Antonio came David Crockett and his group of twelve riflemen from Tennessee. Bowie sized up the Alamo and estimated that it would take at least a thousand men to secure it from an attack by the Mexican army. However, it appeared from the start that Bowie still considered making a stand at the old mission.

Flag of The New Orleans Greys (1835-1836)
Courtesy of The Institute of Texan Cultures, San Antonio

All the while, an enraged Santa Anna, deeply disturbed by the fact that his brother-in-law, Cos, with superior forces surrendered to the Texians, was determined to make amends by punishing the Anglos and taking back the Texas frontier for Mexico. Santa Anna's retaliation would be swift and decisive. By the time Bowie reached the Alamo, Santa Anna was already into Saltillo with his army of around 5,400 men, 21 cannons, 1,800 pack mules, 33 four-wheeled wagons, and 200 two-wheeled carts. Fifteen hundred men under Ramirez y Sesma would represent the vanguard unit who would advance to San Antonio. Additionally, there were the 1,600 men and six guns of Gaona at Saltillo, the 1,800 men and six guns of Tolsa at Monclova, the 437-man cavalry under Andrade, and 300 infantry, 301 lances, and one four-pounder under

36

Don José Urrea, who would proceed to Matamoros, destroy the Texas expedition there, then retake Goliad.

Santa Anna would command the main force in taking San Antonio. Being a military man, he did not care about the weather or roads since his prime objective was to destroy the enemy as quickly as possible—he gave the orders, and the men obeyed. He was poised with a ratification of his Texas campaign by his Congress. Every colonist who took part in the rebellion would be executed or exiled. Those who did not take part would be relocated to the interior. The Texians would pay for his campaign through the reallocation of their lands to his soldiers, and every person bearing arms against Mexico would be considered a traitor.

In this way, Santa Anna set out to exterminate North American influence in Mexican Texas. This was a revolution even by international law and was punishable by extreme measures.

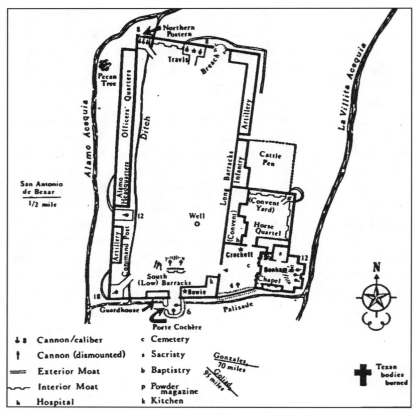

The Alamo as fortified by General Cos
From Fox, Archaeological Investigations in Alamo Plaza,
San Antonio, Bexar County, Texas, 1988-1989 (1995:5)

Martyrdom

God and Texas—Victory or Death!

The close of Travis's last letter from
the Alamo, on March 3, 1836

On February 2, 1836, Bowie decided that the fate of Texas depended on keeping the Alamo out of the hands of the Mexicans. He and Neill and their contingent were willing to die at the Alamo rather than surrender it to the enemy. Luckily for Neill, he was called home on business in mid-February and turned over his command to an eager Travis, who gladly accepted. After the decision to remain was made, only a few simple modifications were undertaken at the Alamo including the digging of a well in the plaza and the construction of a parapet to strengthen the north wall of the plaza.

At the time of the battle, a twelve-foot wall ran west for 50 feet from the northwest corner of the chapel to the barracks, which was a two-story structure. It was 186 feet long by 18 feet wide and 18 feet high; from the northeast corner of the chapel, a wall ran 186 feet north and 102 feet west to connect the long barracks, forming a patio and inner court. A strong stockade, 114 feet by 17 feet long, was constructed from the southwest corner of the chapel to a one-story low barracks and comprising a part of the south wall. Half of the building was used as a prison while the remainder housed the soldiers.

Other one-story buildings formed part of the west wall while the enclosure to the west of the chapel formed a large quadrangle approximately 154 feet by 54 feet long with the north wall longer than the south wall. A messenger, who left the compound prior to the battle, described the chapel's roof as being in ruins from neglect but still representing the strongest building in the compound. The earlier, exposed southeast portion of the smaller yard was now closed by a log palisade and earthenworks, which stretched from the chapel to the south wall.

Santa Anna's army, in its drive toward San Antonio in the winter, faced brutal cold, sparse food, and little water on the trek to destroy the Anglo settlers. The first night after crossing the Rio Grande, fifty oxen froze to death. The days were followed by a trail of abandoned equipment, more dead animals, and straggling soldiers all the way to San Antonio. Santa Anna would not be delayed at any cost since he was on a mission of revenge. He and his army reached the Rio Grande in mid-February due to his phenomenal pace. By the time his army reached the outskirts of Bexar, they had only two batteries of small six-pound cannons. Surprised to discover that the Alamo was being held by a small force of Anglos, Santa Anna immediately set up strategic defensive positions there. The people of Bexar constantly provided him with details about the Anglos including the fact that they had only 150 men defending the Alamo.

The siege of the Alamo did not result in an immediate and decisive victory as Santa Anna had originally anticipated. Inside, the small force of 150 men held out hope that help would eventually reach them—to the very end. Messengers came and went daily attempting to solicit more volunteers and keep Travis apprised of the situation. Travis took over command of the post as Bowie's health was slowly deteriorating. The Alamo defenders had many chances to escape but refused to leave.

Storming of the Alamo
Courtesy of The Institute of Texan Cultures, San Antonio

At 3 A.M. on March 1, reinforcements came to the Alamo. A group of twenty-five men from Gonzales were the only ones to respond to Travis's plea for help. Under George Kimbell and with Deaf Smith guiding them, they rode through Mexican lines into the fortress. Travis knew this was not enough support and sent out another plea delivered by Juan Seguin, "Give me help, oh my Country." Sadly, it was in vain. All the while, the Mexican army grew in size. Still, the rifles of the Alamo defenders made a 200-yard swath around the structure a killing zone. Any Mexican within that range was usually gunned down by the sharp-shooters. Mexican Captain Rafael Soldana remembered a man (probably Crockett) who rarely missed when he fired, always rising to his feet to fire and then calmly reloading his gun, indifferent to the Mexican fire power.

After ten days of siege, Santa Anna was growing impatient. He shelled the Alamo at night to unnerve the men. Attempting to slowly move the cannons within range of the walls, many of the Mexicans were killed by the long rifles. Music played from within the fort as the men waited and the shelling continued. There was little else they could do. Each morning the defenders would look out and see the cannons being maneuvered closer. The walls were taking a greater pounding each day, and shoring them up was becoming useless. Travis noted that as of March 3, at least two hundred shells had fallen inside the compound without killing a single man. That would soon change. While the men inside wrote to their loved ones, most expecting to die, Travis appeared to believe help would eventually arrive. By Friday, March 5, the cannons were only 250 yards away, and the Mexican gunners were firing from 200 yards. The walls were crumbling around the men in the fort, and a pervasive doom settled in. There were no signs of reinforcements—the defenders were alone.

Although Travis told the men they were free to go, only Louis Rose departed the night of March 5. Other myths about the final hours inside the Alamo remain: Did Travis actually draw a line in the sand to see who would join him or leave; did the Texians actually hoist a flag that boasted the numerals "1824" to show they were fighting for the Liberal Constitution and not against the Mexican nation? The only certainties are that Travis, Crockett, Bowie, and the 180-plus men held the Alamo against overwhelming odds for thirteen days ending on March 6, 1836.

Suddenly, at 10 o'clock on Saturday night, March 5, Santa Anna ceased firing. There had hardly been a pause in the cannon fire for eleven days. Finally, the exhausted men were able to sleep. But in the back of their minds, they knew this was the calm before the storm, a brief respite before all hell broke loose—and it did the following morning. That night, Santa Anna made his final plans for the assault in the early hours of Sunday, March 6. At 1 A.M., the men were stirring, and by 4 A.M., they were in position to attack. The moon was obscured by clouds when at 5 A.M. the signal to attack was given, and the Mexican army rushed the Alamo.

Captain John Baugh, manning the wall, shouted the alarm, and in short order the men of the Alamo were firing from every part of the compound. For Travis, this was his moment of glory, one he had hoped for all his life—a life that ended before he reached thirty.

The first frontal assault from the east was pinned down by deadly rifle fire, and Crockett's men stopped the Mexican advance on the south wall. On the north wall, a few soldiers reached the safety of high walls while the rest of the Mexican northern column stopped. Travis, screaming orders from the walls, was hit by a bullet to the head. He lived only a short time after falling down the embankment. The Mexicans regrouped and came a second time and met with the same deadly fire, dead falling upon dead. By the third advance, all three columns merged as a single mass charging toward the walls of the Alamo. A breach did not come instantly, as many more Mexican soldiers were cut down. The break finally occurred at the redoubt that Green Jameson had constructed of earth and timber. At this point, Santa Anna committed his reserves. This was the end for the Alamo defenders.

Once inside the compound, it was hand-to-hand combat described by the Mexicans as a horrible encounter. From the open plaza, the defenders fell back to the long barracks. Mexican soldiers by now were swarming from everywhere. It was every man for himself. Inside the long barracks, the defenders made their last futile stand. The Mexicans with their gleaming bayonets went from building to building until they had killed every man. One

Martyrdom

The Fall of the Alamo
From Gentilz-Fretelliere Family Papers: Photograph from the
Collections of The Daughters of the Republic of Texas Library

defender in particular was described by the Mexican soldiers as being "blessed." He was a tall American of rather dark complexion and wearing a buckskin coat and a round cap made out of fox skin with a long tail hanging down his back. He was fired on repeatedly by the soldiers but was never struck. The defender never missed a shot. In the end, he was finally slashed in the face with a sword and bayoneted by at least twenty men. This man was most likely David Crockett. Jim Bowie held out in his room in the long barracks until he was viciously bayoneted on his cot so many times that his blood covered the Mexican soldiers, staining their clothes crimson.

The last defenders were in the church, which was being bombarded by an 18-pound cannon. Susanna Dickinson, wife of Almeron, and their daughter Angelina, along with a few other women and black slaves were inside. The Mexican soldiers killed Robert Evans as he tried in vain to blow up the magazine. Jacob Walker from Nacogdoches ran into Susanna Dickinson's room and was immediately bayoneted in front of her and her child; then all was quiet.

The Alamo Defenders Dead and Buried

Bexarians! Return to your homes and dedicate yourselves to your domestic duties. Your city and the fortress of the Alamo are already in possession of the Mexican Army, composed of your fellow citizens; and rest assured that no mass of foreigners will ever interrupt your repose, much less attack your lives and plunder your property. The Supreme Government has taken you under its protection and will seek for your good.

King, Santa Anna's letter to Houston (1976:44)

The sun rose ninety minutes after the bugle signaled the attack to begin. In all, between 183 and 189 men were killed including five men who hid themselves and were discovered after the fighting ended. They were subsequently executed.

Travis's slave was asked to identify the bodies of Bowie and Travis. Susanna Dickinson, her daughter, and a handful of women, children, and slaves were spared. The Mexican army lost as many as 1,500 soldiers although the actual number is speculation since Santa Anna had some of the men buried. When the cemetery was full, others were tossed into the river. The loss of up to one-third of his force was of small concern to Santa Anna, for his revenge was complete. Although the battle was insignificant in terms of stopping him, the psychological effect of the Alamo slaughter was comparable to the Greek valor at Thermopylae. The war was not over, only the battle.

A number of published and unpublished accounts from the survivors of the Alamo battle provide information about the dead and buried. Matovina (1995) provides an excellent summary of extant material pertaining to Tejano accounts and perspectives of the battle and the aftermath as obtained through newspaper accounts and reminiscences. The best accounts are attributed to Alamo survivors: Juana Navarro Alsbury, Enrique Esparza, Eulalia Yorba, Susanna Dickinson, and Pablo Diaz.

Based on these accounts, the lists of survivors, though inconsistent, include: Juana Navarro's son, Alejo Perez, and her sister, Gertrudis Navarro; Enrique Esparza's mother, Anna Salazar Esparza, his sister, and three brothers; Mrs. Concepcion Losoya, her daughter, and two sons; Mrs. Victoriana and three little girls; Mrs. Susanna Dickinson and her baby daughter; an old woman named Petra; Mrs. Juana Melton; Trinidad Saucedo, and others as yet not identified by name. Enrique Esparza also attests to the fact that Brigidio Guerrero was spared because he convinced Mexican soldiers that the Texian forces held him prisoner. Groneman (1990) provides a detailed account of the Alamo defenders including a geneology.

The Alamo in 1850
Drawn by Herman Lungkwitz, Rau & Son Lithographers showing the Alamo in ruins
Courtesy of The Institute of Texan Cultures, San Antonio

47

According to Francisco Antonio Ruiz, the alcalde of San Antonio, at 2 P.M. on the twenty-third day of February 1836, General Santa Anna entered the city of San Antonio with a part of his army and encountered no resistance. The forces under the command of Travis, Bowie, and Crockett left on the same day at 8 A.M. after learning that the Mexican army was on the banks of the Medina River. The Texians relocated in the fortress of the Alamo. Both groups exchanged continual artillery and musket fire from February 23 until March 6 when, at 3 P.M., General Santa Anna and four thousand men advanced against the Alamo. The infantry, artillery, and cavalry formed several hundred yards outside the walls of the fortress, and the Mexican army was repulsed twice by the deadly fire of Travis' artillery. On the third charge, the Toluca battalion scaled the walls and suffered severely. Out of 800 men, only 130 were left alive.

When the Mexican army entered the walls, Ruiz with the political chief (jefe politico), Don Ramon Musquiz, and others accompanied the curate, Don Refugio de la Garza, who, by Santa Anna's orders, had assembled during the night a temporary fortification erected in Potrero Street to attend the wounded. As soon as the Mexican troops began storming the Alamo, Ruiz and the others crossed the bridge on Commerce Street to view the attack. They were fired upon by a party of Mexican dragoons and fell back to the river. After a half hour, Santa Anna sent one of his aides-de-camp with orders to come before him. He directed Ruiz to call on neighbors to carry the dead to the cemetery. Santa Anna also had Ruiz and the others point out Colonels Travis, Bowie, and Crockett.

The body of Travis was found on the north battery of the Alamo on the gun carriage, shot only in the forehead. Toward the west and in the small fort opposite the city, the body of Crockett was found. Bowie was found dead in his bed in one of the rooms on the south side. After all the Mexicans were taken out, Santa Anna ordered wood to be brought to burn the bodies of the Texians. He sent a company of dragoons with Ruiz to gather the wood and dry branches from the nearby forest. Around three in the afternoon, kindling materials were laid out, and the bodies were placed on top. Additional wood was then piled on the bodies, all arranged in layers. Kindling wood was placed throughout the pile, and it was lit at around five in the evening. The dead Mexicans of Santa Anna were taken to the graveyard, but lacking room for them, some were thrown into the river on the same day. Santa Anna's losses were estimated at 1,600 men. According to Ruiz, the gallantry of the Alamo defenders was admired by the Mexican army. Even the generals were astonished at their vigorous resistance and how dearly victory had been bought. Ruiz recorded the burning of 182 men.

Another account of the March 6 battle comes from Enrique Esparza, who claimed to be the only remaining survivor of the siege when his story was published in May 1907, in the *San Antonio Express.* Esparza was twelve years old when the Alamo fell—an event forever etched in his mind. He was born the son of Gregorio Esparza, a man listed as dying in the Alamo. His mother, Anna Salazar Esparza, and some of his brothers and a sister also witnessed the massacre. After Santa Anna arrived, the Esparza's, who were friends of the Texians, moved out of Bexar and into the Alamo in the early evening of the first day of the siege.

Esparza remembered that all of the doors were closed and barred and that sentinels were posted upon the roof, protected by the walls of the Alamo church and the old convent building. The family was admitted into the church through a small window where several cannons were positioned. Some were behind the doors while others were mounted on the roof and in the convent. As a child, Esparza recalled being frightened by the cannon fire that roared between both sides, some shots rattling the chapel and convent.

Esparza, though not given a weapon because weapons and ammunition were scarce, remembered seeing children his age or younger fighting and dying as bravely as the adults. Men, women, and children died defending the Alamo, and although he did not count the days, the nights were long and full of terror. He reminisced about Crockett's leadership and the fact that he was everywhere, personally directing the fighting. Travis was in command, but he relied more on Crockett's judgment than his own. Bowie was brave, but he was ill and lying in his cot unable to see what was happening around him. Although he was too weak to stand, when Travis drew the line with his sword [this action has been repeatedly questioned from a historical standpoint] Bowie had his cot carried across the line.

Crockett was called "Don Benito" by several Mexicans. Esparza remembered that a message was delivered by Santa Anna allowing those inside to leave if they wished— quite a number of civilians left. He recalled names like Menchaca, Flores, Rodriguez, Ramirez, Arocha, and Silvero exiting during the armistice; Louis "Moses" Rose, the lone defender to leave the Alamo, departed at night sometime between March 3 and March 6. Esparza's father said he would stay and die fighting, and his mother vowed to stay with him to the end with the children.

According to Esparza, the end came suddenly and with a rush. In the early hours of the morning of March 6, a cannon boomed and a shot crashed through the doors and windows and breaches in the walls. Then the Mexican soldiers swarmed over everyone, firing in volleys and striking the defenders down with their muskets. Esparza recalled an American boy about his own age who rose to his feet and stood calmly and unarmed as he was killed, the boy's corpse falling over Esparza.

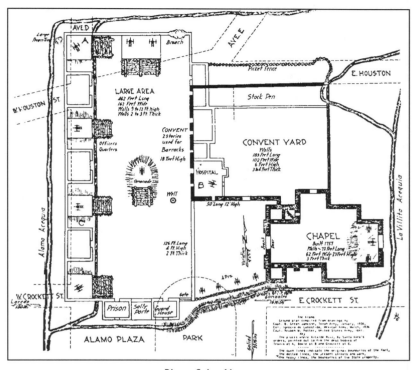

Plan of the Alamo
Compiled from drawings by Green Jameson (1836), Colonel Ignacio de Labastida (1836) and Captain Reuben M. Potter (1841). Map on file, DRT Library, The Alamo

The body of Esparza's father lay near the cannon he tended. Esparza's mother and baby sister knelt beside it. Behind his mother crouched the only man who escaped and was permitted to surrender: Brigidio Guerrero. The Mexican soldiers stopped when they saw Esparza's mother. Brigidio Guerrero pled for mercy, telling the Mexican soldiers that he was a prisoner in the Alamo. They took Esparza, his mother, sister, and brothers to another part of the building where other women and children all huddled. Esparza noted Mrs. Dickinson and her child, an old woman called Dona Petra, a young girl named Trinidad Saucedo, Mrs. Juana Navarro Alsbury and her sister, and several other women, young girls, and boys. After Santa Anna's soldiers put all the women and children in a corner, the soldiers kept firing into the corpses of the Alamo defenders for a quarter of an hour.

The old convent had been used for barracks by the men under Bowie, Travis, and Crockett's command. It was also a defensive position until Santa Anna's army breached the walls of the convent and drove the defenders to the long barracks for a final stand. Communication was continually kept between the convent and the church building through a door connecting them, and Crockett stayed there for some time until finally being killed in front of the large double doors that he defended with his men. The lifeless body of Crockett was surrounded by a number of dead Mexican soldiers, some of whom he had killed.

The Alamo circa 1868
Exterior of the Alamo during the time it served as United States Quartermaster Depot
Courtesy of The Institute of Texan Cultures, San Antonio

When the Mexican soldiers made their final charge at Bowie, he rose up in his bed and buried his bowie knife into the breast of one of the soldiers as another soldier shot and killed him. Bowie's body was found riddled with bullets. Esparza saw Bowie's corpse before it was taken from the building. After the battle the remaining women and children were kept in the church's southwest corner in the small room to the right of the large double entry door of the church, which was under guard. Eventually, they were brought before Santa Anna and ultimately released. Esparza said that his uncle, Francisco Esparza, was granted permission to search for the body of his brother (Enrique Esparza's father) and upon finding it, was allowed to bury the body in the camposanto (cemetery) where Milam Square is now located.

Another Alamo battle narrative came from Eulalia Yorba, who was thirty-four years old when the Alamo was besieged. During an interview with a *San Francisco Examiner* reporter, she told of how everyone in Bexar was apprised hourly of the siege. Although the local inhabitants learned that the Texians had been given four days to surrender, the Mexican soldiers related that not one of the defenders had responded to the demand for surrender and that on the morning of the sixth of March, Santa Anna was planning to bring matters to a head with the rebel forces. Yorba told of the anxiety that all the people on the outside felt for that mere handful of men in the old fort with hostile troops visible everywhere and no help available.

Continuing, Yorba said that the morning of Sunday, March 6 was a day she could never forget. It was clear and balmy, and every scrap of food was gone from her house. Yorba and the children ran to the home of an old Spanish priest where they could obtain food and shelter. There was nothing to hinder the view of the Alamo from the priest's home although Yorba wished there was. The shooting began at six in the morning with a multitude of soldiers with guns swarming the stone building. Volley after volley was fired into the barred and bolted windows. Then the volleys came in quick succession. Occasionally, Yorba heard muffled volleys and saw puffs of smoke from within the Alamo, and when Mexican soldiers were seen falling in the roadway or staggering back, everyone knew the Texians were fighting for their lives. It seemed as if ten thousand guns were shot off randomly, sounding like firecrackers snapping all at once. The smoke grew thick, and Yorba's group could not clearly see the Alamo as the din of musketry and screams of crazy, exultant Mexicans increased every moment. Yorba said she never heard human beings scream so fiercely and powerfully as the Mexican soldiers did that day, likening the sound to a yell of a panther in desperate straits.

Next, Yorba recalled several companies of soldiers running down the street with great heavy bridge timbers. These were quickly brought to bear as battering rams on the mission doors, but several volleys from within the Alamo stopped the battering for a short time. Three or four brass cannons were loaded and placed directly in front of the main doors of the mission; they did serious damage. Meanwhile, bullets from several thousand muskets incessantly rained like hail upon the building and went through the apertures made in the wood barricades at the windows and doors. The din was indescribable. It did not seem as if a mouse could live in a building so shot at and riddled as the Alamo was that morning. Yorba saw ladders brought in three times in an attempt to scale the low roof of the church, which was crowded with a screaming throng of men armed with guns and sabers.

Yorba remembered that the priest drew the family away from the window and refused to let them look any longer; however, they could still hear the shouts as cannon fire shook the priest's house and rattled the windowpanes. About nine o'clock the shooting and yelling ceased, but the air was thick and heavy with blue powder smoke. A Mexican colonel came running to the priest's residence and asked that they all go immediately to the Alamo and do what they could for the dying men. Yorba and the family followed the priest and were faced with a dreadful sight. The roadway was thronged with Mexican soldiers with smoke-smudged faces, haggard eyes, and wild, insane expressions. Many Mexicans lay dead or dying while others were being carried to an adobe house.

The stones in the church wall were spotted with blood; the doors were splintered and battered in. Pools of thick blood were so frequent on the ground around the stone building that care had to be taken to avoid stepping in them. There was a din of excited voices along the street, and the officers were marshaling their men for moving to camp. But no one could even describe the carnage of the scene when everyone reached the inside of the Alamo and faced a sympathetic colonel who allowed them to bandage up the wounds of several young men there. Yorba said that when she was younger, she used to try and describe the horror she witnessed but could never find sufficient language. There were only a few Mexicans in there when she came, and they were all officers who had ordered the common soldiers away from the scene of death and slaughter. The floor was literally crimson with blood. The woodwork all about the dead was riddled and splintered by lead balls, and what was left of the old altar at the rear of the church was cut and slashed by cannon fire and bullets. The air was laden with gunpowder smoke, and the odor was oppressive and sickening.

The dead Texians lay alone or in piles, strewn about the floor of the Alamo, just as they had fallen. Yorba and the others went to work as soon as they arrived to help the dying men who had only a short time to live. So thick were the bodies of the dead that Yorba remembers having to step over them to get [near] a man who was still alive. Close to her feet was a young man who had been shot through the forehead. He had dropped dead with his eyes staring wildly open, and as he lay there, he seemingly gazed up into Yorba's face. She remembers seeing Colonel Davy Crockett as he lay dead by the side of a dying man whose bloody and powder-stained face she was washing. Colonel Crockett was about fifty years old, and his coat and rough woolen shirt were so soaked with blood that the original color was hidden, as the hero must have died from a shot to the chest or a bayonet thrust.

Another tale came from Juan Seguin as he spoke of how he gathered the bones of the defenders from the funeral pyres after the battle and buried them near the altar of the San Fernando Cathedral. Unfortunately, Seguin contradicted this story on another occasion by stating that after the battle, he collected bones from the cremation sites near the battlefield in 1837, placed them in coffins, and paraded them through San Antonio's main thoroughfare before returning them to a cremation site for burial with military honors. Such stories obscure the truth as to where the actual remains of the defenders lie: near the altar of the Mission San Fernando Cathedral or on the battlefield somewhere near the Alamo.

Another account of the fall of the Alamo was taken from Meyers (1896), who conducted interviews with various people who recalled the battle and summarized their accounts in a pamphlet entitled "History, Battles and Fall of the Alamo with Points of Interest, Etc., of San Antonio Texas." The pamphlet describes how just prior to the battle a stillness like death prevailed over the area. Those who remember the battle, recall being about a quarter mile from the action and hearing the constant thunder of the

The Alamo circa 1878
Engraving by Rand McNally; Courtesy of The Institute of Texan Cultures, San Antonio

bombardment from Santa Anna's force and the responding fire from the Alamo defenders. The firing continued until a little before sunrise on the morning of the sixth when it ceased.

A Sergeant Becerra described the preparations for the final assault by saying, "On the third of March, General Tolza arrived. The greatest activity prevailed in every department. The plan of assault was formed and communicated to the commander of corps and others on the fifth. On the same day, ammunition, scaling ladders, etc. were distributed. Everything was made ready for the storming. During the night, troops were placed in position. About three o'clock on the morning of the sixth, the battalion, Matamoros, was marched to a point near the river and above the Alamo. In their rear were two thousand men under Generals Cos and Castrillon, who commanded this part of the army. Tolza's command held the ground below the Alamo."

According to Becerra, General Santa Anna spent the night contemplating the battle not far from the Alamo. The troops were to march to the attack when the bugler at headquarters sounded the advance. The bugle was sounded at 4 A.M. on March 6. The troops under General Castrillon moved in silence and, upon reaching the fort, planted scaling ladders and commenced ascending, some mounted on the shoulders of others. A terrible fire belched from the interior. Men fell from the scaling ladders by the score; many pierced through the head by gunshot, others clubbed to death. The dead and wounded covered the ground. After half an hour of fierce conflict and the sacrifice of many lives, the column of General Castrillon succeeded in making a lodgement in the upper part of the Alamo to the northeast. Becerra thought that the area was now used as a lot or courtyard. This seeming advantage was a mere prelude to the desperate struggle that ensued. The doors of the Alamo building were barricaded by bags of sand as high as the neck of a man—the windows also. On the top of the roofs of the different apartments were rows of sandbags to cover the besieged.

The Mexican troops, inspired by success, continued the attack with energy and boldness. The Texians fought like devils. It was at short range, muzzle to muzzle, hand to hand, musket and rifle, bayonet and bowie knife—all were mingled in confusion: here a squad of Mexicans, there a Texian or two. The crash of firearms, the shouts of defiance, the cries of the dying and wounded made a din almost infernal. The Texians desperately defended every inch of the fort. Overpowered by numbers, they would be forced to abandon a room. They would rally in the next and defend it until further resistance became impossible. General Tolza's troops forced an entrance at the door of the church building. He met the same determined resistance without and within. He won by force of numbers and a great sacrifice of life. There was a long, darkened room on the ground floor (long barracks). Here the fight was bloody: It proved to be the hospital. Becerra's detachment had captured an artillery piece and placed it near the door of the hospital, doubly charged with grape and canister; it was fired twice. Becerra and his men entered and found the corpses of fifteen Texians. On the outside, forty-two Mexican soldiers were found dead. On the top of the church building, Becerra saw eleven Texans. They had small pieces of artillery and were firing on the cavalry and on those engaged in making the escalade. Their ammunition was exhausted, and they were loading with pieces of iron and nails. The captured piece was placed in a position to reach them, doubly charged, and fired with so much effect that they ceased working their pieces.

Fort Alamo
Courtesy of The Institute of Texan Cultures, San Antonio

59

Becerra believed that at least two of the men killed were Travis and Crockett, though he admitted he did not know them personally and might be mistaken as to their identities. After the battle, General Santa Anna directed Colonel Mora to send out his cavalry to collect wood in order to burn the bodies of the Texians; their remains became offensive and were collected and buried afterward by Colonel Juan Seguin. According to Becerra, the Mexican dead and wounded presented a frightful sight. The dead soldiers littered the ground surrounding the Alamo. The bodies were heaped inside the Alamo where blood and brains covered the ground and stained the walls. The ghastly faces of the fallen Mexicans met the gaze of the living, and their bodies were removed with great sadness. The loss of Mexican life was estimated by Becerra to be roughly two thousand killed and more than three hundred wounded.

The Alamo
From the San Antonio Conservation Society, King William Strasse
Courtesy of The Institue of Texan Cultures, San Antonio

Those killed during the battle were generally struck on the head, the neck, or the shoulder, seldom below that. The firing of the Texian defenders was precise. When a Texian rifle was leveled on a Mexican, he was considered as good as dead. All this indicates the bravery of the men who were engaged in a hopeless conflict with an enemy outnumbering them more than twenty to one. They inflicted on the Mexican army a loss ten times greater than they envisioned. The victory of the Alamo was obtained at a high price. The number of Texian dead was never accurately ascertained. It included all the volunteers and at least twenty to twenty-five Mexicans who joined the Texians. Mrs. Candelaria, Colonel Bowie's nurse (although the fact that she was at the Alamo at the time of the battle has since been disputed), gives the names of four Mexicans who were alive when the Alamo fell or were killed fighting. Mrs. Alsbury in her statement mentions the killing of one Mexican after Santa Anna's army entered the Alamo. The Texians loss in the siege is not positively known. It was certainly fewer than two hundred.

A Doctor Sutherland attempted to learn the exact loss sustained by the Mexican army at San Antonio. He stated that the messenger who was sent by the Navarro family at San Antonio, four days after the fall, reported the enemy's loss to have been about fifteen hundred. Sutherland visited Santa Anna after he was made prisoner at San Jacinto. He questioned Santa Anna's private secretary as to the number of men in the army at San Antonio and the number killed in battle. The secretary replied that the army consisted of five thousand men of whom fifteen hundred and forty-four of the army's best were lost fighting. He concluded that the Texians "fought more like devils than men."

An interview with Juan Antonio Chavez is documented in the *San Antonio Express* for April 19, 1914.

During the interview, Chavez detailed the burial of human remains after the fall of the Alamo. According to Chavez, when the battle took place, Chavez was only a boy, yet he remembered certain details. The Chavez family had experienced another battle during the December 1835 siege when Ben Milam and his men captured San Antonio from General Cos. When the Chavez family returned to their ranch on Calaveras Creek, fifteen miles from this city, they found their home almost completely destroyed by the battle. The structure was riddled by cannon fire and bullets.

Once again, the Chavez family was forced to relocate to their ranch in February 1836 as Santa Anna's forces moved into town. They remained there until the battle of the Alamo was over. When the family returned, the bodies of those who had perished in the Alamo were still burning on two immense pyres on the old Alameda. As a boy, Chavez remembered going over to see the funeral pyres, a sight that left an indelible impression in his memory. According to Chavez, one pyre occupied a position on the site where the Halff building is. The other was diagonally across the street on what is now known as the lawn of the Ludlow House and the house adjoining it on the east.

The bodies burned for several days, and the wood and tallow fuel used for consuming them were frequently replenished. Chavez made several trips to the scene, which so fascinated him that he could not stay away until all of the bodies had been consumed. The bodies were all reduced to ashes except a few charred heads, arms, and legs that were scattered about. These were gathered up and placed in a shallow grave where the Ludlow House lawn was in 1914. Continuing, Chavez commented that all of the officers and some of the privates of Santa Anna's army were buried in the cemetery where Milam Park now is, but the slain Mexicans were so numerous, it was thought the quickest and best way of disposing of the bodies was to throw them into the San Antonio River, which was then a swift and deep stream. However, there were so many bodies that they choked its flow. Many of them lodged in the curves of the river.

During the course of a July 1, 1906 interview for the *San Antonio Express*, ninety-year-old Pablo Diaz described the aftermath of the Alamo battle. For Diaz, to have seen the ashes of the slain Alamo defenders was an experience few people could claim. He recalled the place where the heroes' corpses were burned as well as a description of where the few remaining charred bones were interred. According to Diaz, he came to San Antonio February 18, not long after Austin and Burleson and their forces came to the vicinity of San Antonio and located their camp near the head of the San Antonio River and later at the Molino Blanco. Around that time, Captain Juan N. Seguin was recruiting men to join Austin's force of American colonists. Seguin prevailed on Pablo's brother, Francisco, to enlist in his company; however, Pablo thought better of taking up arms against the Mexicans, remaining neutral throughout the conflict.

After General Cos surrendered in December 1835, the Texian army that remained in San Antonio resided in the barracks vacated by the Mexicans on Military Plaza. When Davy Crockett arrived, the men moved to the Alamo because the defenses were more substantial than the ones on the west side of the city. The weakness of the Military Plaza, or the Presidio, as it was called, had been demonstrated by the ease with which Milam's forces dislodged the soldiers under General Cos. The arrival of Santa Anna was announced by the firing of a cannon in front of the alcalde's [mayor's] house on Main Plaza. Santa Anna's red flag was hoisted over the cathedral, which meant that no quarter would be shown those opposing him. This was well understood by those in the Alamo.

Diaz recalled hearing the roar of the cannons and shots being fired continuously during the siege, and he did not leave the protection of the mission for fear that he would become involved in the terrible slaughter which he knew would occur. Messengers frequently came to the mission and told Cruz and others of the terrible devastation and butchery in progress and of the brave and dauntless defense by the heroic Constitutionalists. The cannon shots became louder and more frequent as Santa Anna's soldiers moved in closer to the Alamo. Finally, on the sixth day, after a fierce fusillade, there was silence, and Diaz saw the red flag of Santa Anna floating from the Alamo where the Constitutional flag before had been. He knew that the battle was over. He had several personal friends among the brave men in the Alamo including a man named Cervantes whose descendants had lived on the Alameda for many years.

The Alamo circa 1868
Photograph by Doerr. Courtesy of The Institute of Texan Cultures, San Antonio

64

The next sight Diaz remembered was an immense pillar of flame shooting up a short distance to the south and east of the Alamo with dense smoke rising high into the clouds. The fire burned for two days and nights, and then flames and smoke subsided and smoldered. Diaz left his place of refuge and approached the Alamo from along Garden Street. He immediately noticed that the air was tainted with the terrible odor from many corpses, and he witnessed hundreds of vultures circling above him. As Diaz reached the ford of the river, he saw that the stream was clogged with the corpses that had been thrown into it. The alcalde, Francisco Antonio Ruiz, had vainly attempted to bury the bodies of the Mexican soldiers who had been slain by the Alamo defenders. Ruiz had exhausted all of his resources and was still unable to find space to bury the remaining men. Thousands of Santa Anna's soldiers had fallen before they annihilated their adversaries and captured the fortress. A horrified Diaz turned aside but could not help seeing corpses everywhere he turned. The river was congested from the bend in the river (Garden Street to above Commerce Street) to as far as Crockett Street is today. The bodies stayed there for many days until Ruiz managed to dislodge them and float them down the river. But while this was a most gruesome sight, the one Diaz saw later filled him with more horror.

Diaz continued to the Alameda, which at the time was a broad and spacious, irregularly shaped place, flanked on both sides with huge cottonwood trees (from which it gets its name). He turned into the Alameda at the present intersection of Commerce and Alamo Streets. Looking east, he witnessed a large crowd and instinctively went to see the cause of the commotion. There, he saw the remains of the fallen heroes just beyond where the Ludlow now stands. The crowd was gathered around the smoldering embers and ashes of the fire that he had witnessed from the mission. It was here that Ruiz had ordered the bodies of Bowie, Crockett, Travis, and all of their comrades to be brought and burned. Fragments of flesh, bones, and charred wood and ashes revealed the terrible truth. Oil that had exuded from the bodies saturated the earth for several feet beyond the ashes and smoldering mesquite embers. The odor was far more sickening than that from the corpses in the river. Diaz turned his head aside and left the place.

Diaz took the reporter to the exact spot where the bodies were burned near the old Post House. This was the same location pointed out to the reporter by another person. Diaz said that the pyre was a very long one as it had to consume nearly two hundred corpses, and it may be that some of the bodies may not have been burned in the main pyre but on the opposite side of the Alameda. Diaz never recalled seeing another pyre or pile of ashes there; however, he was not prepared to state emphatically that no bodies were burned anywhere but at the spot he was about to show the interviewer. It is probable, according to Diaz, that not all of the bodies were carried away from the Alamo concurrently nor were the Alamo defenders all separated from the Mexican soldiers at the same time, so perhaps some of the bodies were burned on the south side of the Alameda where the Springfield House stands. As the story goes, Diaz maintained that the main funeral pyre was about two hundred yards east of St. Joseph's church and just beyond the Ludlow House and from there, fifty to sixty yards north.

Eventually, Diaz and the reporter reached the spot and pointed to a location confirmed by a man named Perez, who stated that, as a little boy while playing on the Alameda, he was frequently shown the same spot as the place where the bodies of the Alamo heroes were burned. Perez went further than Diaz, stating that for many years there was a small mound there under which he was told that the charred bones the fire did not consume were buried by a humane person who had to do so secretly. He was familiar with the spot as being the burial place of Bowie and Crockett. Perez stated that about thirty years before, these bones were exhumed and placed in the old city cemetery, the first one located on the Powder House Hill, but he did not know the part of the cemetery they were placed in.

In his memoirs (Matovina 1995:113-115), José Maria Rodriguez recalled the Alamo battle and the aftermath. Rodriguez and his parents lived in the first house after crossing the river coming from the Alamo. They entertained Colonel Travis when his small garrison took over the Alamo. It was during this time that Rodriguez's father found out that General Santa Anna was heading toward San Antonio with a large army composed of cavalry, infantry, and artillery. The message was relayed to Colonel Travis with a warning to abandon the Alamo. Travis did not believe the information and chose to remain at the fortress.

Rodriguez maintained that he and his family had to leave Bexar because Santa Anna was coming there (his father joined Sam Houston's army in the meantime). Moving to another house further from the action, Rodriguez and others remember seeing the flash of guns and hearing the cannons roar—the firing lasted about two hours. According to Rodriguez, the next day he heard that all the Texians had been killed and the Alamo taken by Santa Anna's forces. Rodriguez recalled that there was a great deal of discussion with regard to the bodies of the Texians who were slain in the Alamo. Colonel Seguin claimed in a letter that he gathered the ashes of the Alamo defenders the following February, placed them in an iron urn, and buried them in San Fernando Cathedral. Rodriguez questioned this because something like that could not have

The Alamo in the 1870s
From Captain T.K. Treadwell, Bryan, Texas.
Courtesy of The Institute of Texan Cultures, San Antonio

happened without his knowledge. Apparently, Seguin did not return from Houston's army until Rodriquez's father did, both of them being in the same command. The truth is, bones were deposited somewhere in the area near or a little east of where the Menger Hotel is situated now and were buried by Colonel Seguin; however, he does not believe that any remains were buried in the cathedral. Months later, José Maria and his father visited the Alamo and saw blood still on the walls.

King (1976) discusses the fall of the Alamo from the perspective of Susanna Dickinson. As the Mexican soldiers entered Bowie's room, Bowie killed two of the Mexican soldiers with his pistols before they pierced him with their sabers. His slave, Joe, added that Bowie was shot several times through the head, his brains spattering on the wall near his bedside (the marks were still visible on the wall until it was plastered over many years later). Susanna's husband, Almeron Dickinson, during the last throes of the battle, rushed in and told his wife that the Mexicans were

68

The Alamo
Photograph of the interior of the Alamo chapel
before the present roof was installed.
From the San Antonio Conservation Society, King William Strasse
Courtesy of The Institute of Texan Cultures, San Antonio

inside the walls and, if they spared her, "to love Angelina." He then left the church.

Three unarmed Texians entered the room and were shot. Jacob Walker came in followed by four Mexicans who shot him and raised his body with their bayonets. The women and children were forced into a corner of the chapel, and gunshots continued to be heard for a quarter of an hour.

Susanna Dickinson was brought before General Castrillon, who took her to Santa Anna. On her way, she was shot in the calf. At the same time, she saw Crockett's body between the chapel and the long barracks—his coonskin cap lying next to his body. After receiving a letter from Santa Anna to take to General Houston, Susanna left the massacre to deliver the message, not returning to the Alamo until Wednesday, April 27, 1881—forty-five years after she left.

In the small dark room in the rear of the chapel with only a candle to light the darkened space, Susanna recognized almost every stone including the arch overhead, and she spoke with tears in her eyes. Memories flooded her consciousness as she pointed to where the couch once stood and the window through which she watched the blood of the defenders seep into the ground.

After the fall of the Alamo, General Andrade passed by the fortress on his way back to Mexico with an order to dismantle it. He apparently leveled all single walls and filled in the fosse ditch; he dismantled and burned the picket barricade in front of the church along the south wall and around the gate. A plan of the entire mission compound was drawn by Lieutenant Edward Everett in 1846. In 1848 the U.S. Army occupied the Alamo and spent the next few years clearing the rubble, leveling the area, making major repairs to the structures, and making it into a serviceable granary.

The walls of the low stone barracks and old prison building appeared to still be standing at this time. By 1871 the clearing of the plaza, including removing the walls of a shed, was completed. The plaza was scraped and leveled, which removed or scrambled most of the archaeological evidence from prior periods to create better drainage as well as clean up the plaza area. In 1889, when mesquite block paving was laid in the plaza, the wall footings were again exposed and no doubt damaged to an even greater extent. At this time, topsoil was spread over the area and a park created which remains today.

Archaeology: The Alamo and Plaza

The excavations in front of the Alamo shrine provided the opportunity to examine a portion of the building foundation as well as to sample the relatively undisturbed soils which lie adjacent. The stratified soils tested provided a variety of datable artifacts which represent some of the most important past events which occurred at the Alamo.

Jack Eaton, *Excavations at the Alamo Shrine, Mission San Antonio de Valero* (1990:1)

A number of prior archaeological investigations and excavations have been conducted on the grounds of the Alamo since the 1960s, and the results have confirmed that remains dating back to the initial construction of the mission through to the defense of the Alamo still remain intact below the existing ground surface.

An excellent summary of prior archaeological work on the Alamo grounds and in Alamo Plaza is provided by Anne Fox in Hard (1994:52-56). Beginning in 1966, seven areas within the courtyards were excavated by John Greer (1967) for the State Building Commission and the Witte Museum after artifacts were discovered during the installation of electric lines. The data yielded architectural and archaeological information about the methods used in the construction of the Grenet store, the Spanish army, and Spanish mission buildings. These features included a flagstone floor relating to the mission workrooms, footings of a wall which separated the courtyards, pavement in the

71

Excavations in front of the Alamo looking north
From Eaton, Excavations at the Alamo Shrine (1980:56)
Courtesy of The Center for Archaeological Research, The University of Texas at San Antonio

southwest corner of the convent courtyard, and the adobe foundation of a building that appeared to precede the present convento.

During the summer of 1970, excavations by William W. Sorrow in the area south of the chapel where an addition to the DRT Library was about to be built revealed footings of 1800s brick store buildings that once existed in the area as well as discovering evidence that a stone lining of the acequia, which ran east of the chapel, was added after its first construction. Additional excavation was conducted by Mardith Schuetz in 1973 at the east end of the north courtyard. The testing located early foundations against the east courtyard wall as well as the original line of the north wall. In the same year, Fox et al. (1976) investigated the area east of the museum building in the vicinity of Sorrow's acequia discovery in connection with park renovation plans.

Excavations at the Alamo
From Hard, A Historical Overview of Alamo Plaza and Camposanto (1994:53)
Courtesy of The Center for Archaeological Research, The University of Texas at San Antonio

Excavations in Alamo Plaza during 1975 were aimed at determining how much evidence pertaining to the south wall of the mission compound and its related buildings was still preserved. The results indicated that earlier modifications to the plaza had greatly disturbed the subsurface deposits including practically all the south wall of the original Alamo compound. However, archaeologists were able to locate footings and other remnants of the structure.

Jack Eaton (1980) directed excavations in 1977 in the front of the church at its southwest corner. The church footings were recorded, and one end of the wooden palisade wall constructed by General Cos extending from the chapel to the east end of the low barracks was also discovered. Additionally, in 1977 Anne Fox monitored backhoe trenching by city crews outside the west wall of the long barracks and confirmed that the building rests on its original foundation. The monitoring phase also detailed the wall construction and recorded a soil profile of the area. The profile revealed that the upper fifty centimeters of soil consisted of sandy fill containing artifacts from the nineteenth century, followed by five centimeters of brown, sterile clay, three centimeters of deteriorated wall plaster, seventy centimeters of dark brown clay containing colonial period artifacts, and, finally, a layer of tan gravelly soil.

Excavations at the Alamo
From Hard, A Historical Overview of Alamo Plaza and Camposanto (1994:53)
Courtesy of The Center for Archaeological Research, The University of Texas at San Antonio

During 1979 and 1980, James Ivey (1980) excavated an area planned for the Paseo del Rio Park, located across the west wall of the Alamo. A number of eighteenth- and nineteenth-century features were unearthed and recorded including the original adobe west wall of the compound, foundations of later nineteenth century commercial buildings, as well as related subsurface features. The data were used in reconstructing colonial wall lines visible in the park as well as confirming a theory that the direction of the acequia was probably changed by General Cos in 1835 to a point outside the west wall of the mission.

In 1988 a University of Texas at San Antonio field school (under the direction of Fred Valdez) excavated in the area of the defensive lunette south of the mission gate. A major portion of the lunette trench was recorded during this testing program (Fox, 1992; Hard 1994). Joel Gunn in 1989 tested the western edge of Alamo Plaza East directly in line with the defensive trench recorded during 1988. The lunette trench was subsequently discovered. Eighteenth- and nineteenth-century artifacts were discovered twenty to thirty centimeters below street pavement. Finally, Alton Briggs in 1992 directed testing in the area of the museum/gift shop as well as beneath the building in preparation for enlarging the basement where he discovered the east wall of the colonial convento. Only one human skull was recovered from all the testing and monitoring that has occurred over the years, and this was found during the 1979 excavations in the north courtyard.

Speculations on Burials

Even when a building earns a reputation for being haunted, manifestations do not occur all the time. In some instances, certain individuals may set off the phenomenon, as if there is an emotional empathy between it and them. Perhaps during times of inactivity at a haunted place, the phenomenon is there but dormant. Such places may lie at a point where the "veil" between our world and the next is finer, allowing easier access for spirits and demons. These places could be conceived as gateways. Unconsciously, perhaps, psychically gifted people have the ability to open these gates, allowing entry from the other side.

Jenny Randles and Peter Hough, *The Afterlife* (1993)

Archaeologists and historians have been interested in discovering physical evidence for the location of the cemetery and burials associated with the mission as well as the Alamo battle for a number of years. Numerous methods have been considered including those of a scientific nature such as ground penetrating radar, electrical resistivity, and electromagnetic conductivity surveys, in addition to traditional intrusive methods, such as augering, coring, probing, excavation, and geochemical applications. Even nonscientific techniques such as dowsing and using psychics have been tried.

Locating the cemetery to date has proved elusive. Archaeologists believe that if a cemetery or burials exist, they should be encountered in a soil zone referred to as Houston Black Clay which exists in and around the Alamo at a depth of two to five feet below the present ground surface. It is conjectured that this stratum may have only minimal post-burial disturbances; therefore, burials that are known to exist within and adjacent to the chapel area of the present-day Alamo and related to the mission period are believed to still be intact but as yet undiscovered. The burials related to the defense of the Alamo in 1836 of both Anglo and Mexican soldiers is more problematic due to the sparse or conflicting historical data pertaining to the actual burial location(s). Much of this information has been discussed in an earlier chapter entitled The Alamo Defenders: Dead and Buried.

As part of early Christian funeral beliefs, martyrdom ensured that the soul would find heaven; therefore, cemeteries became a focal point of the community. The final resting place of the body was extremely important as were the burial rituals. Secrecy during Roman times resulted in burying the dead in catacombs below the city. By the late 1200s, burials were allowed within a church structure with the rules involved in the burial customs becoming very specific. Interments of non-canonized individuals had to be buried at least one yard from the altar. Furthermore, no infidels or excommunicated persons could be buried in consecrated ground. Although burial within the church was slowly phased out, the practice continued into the eighteenth century.

Early excavations by archaeologists into Spanish missions throughout the southwest and west confirmed the fact that most members of the congregation were buried within and immediately in front of the church, including the entrance, baptistery, and nave, but not in the sanctuary. In some cases, burials were found approximately two feet below the church floor. A Christian burial meant placement of the body within hallowed ground and as close to the church as possible. As time passed and the areas closest to the church became filled, other areas surrounding the church were selected and utilized.

Over the years of excavation and collection of data pertaining to burial practices during Spanish times, the preferred burial location was within the church, with the nave offering the greatest potential area. With the inherent restrictions in adequate burial space came more loosely enforced burial practices. In some cases, cemetery plots were rented, and dereliction of payment resulted in the removal of the coffin and the unceremonious dumping of its contents behind the cemetery without regard to sanitation or fear of disease.

As the times changed, so did the burial customs and practices, as much out of necessity as policy. As the area closest to the church became filled, other areas that were to be designated as hallowed had to be located. With the overcrowding of dead parishioners came the establishment of the camposanto, or cemetery, near the church. The burial practice included placing the dead in front of the church with the feet of the body facing the church while the priests were buried in position to face their congregation. Although the common location for the camposanto was as near to the church as possible and preferably in front and enclosed by walls, some cases required the cemetery to be placed to the side of the church due to the configuration of the church and associated buildings.

Burial records for Mission San Antonio de Valero yield data from the original site in 1718 as well as for the church constructed at its present location in 1724. Between 1724 and 1749, 465 burials were recorded (422 Indians, 26 Spanish, and 17 "unknown"). From 1749 to 1782, 489 burials are recorded (444 Indian, 14 Spanish, 4 mulatto, and 27 "unknown"). In all, 954 burials were recorded as being associated with the first stone church and the present-day church. Parishioners as well as some of the

The Alamo in the 1880s
Catholic Archives, Austin, Texas
Courtesy of The Institute of Texan Cultures, San Antonio

garrison men and hospital patients may have continued to be buried in the camposanto until at least 1807 although military records indicate that most military personnel occupying the mission from 1808 to 1835 were interred in the camposanto located in Bexar (now Milam Park).

Although archaeological research and excavation work in the Alamo and Alamo Plaza have been unable to locate any burials, this can be attributed more to where excavation has been allowed to proceed rather than testing archaeological assumptions based on research. The archaeologists' time has not yet come. However, the two cemetery location theories suggest that, based on traditional church practices, the burials recorded after 1749 should be located either adjacent to the convento (now the long barracks museum) within what is now Alamo Street East facing south or at the south end of the convento directly in front of the church of San Antonio de Valero (presently referred to as the Alamo Shrine).

Either theory would place the location of the early cemetery in front of the church and possibly into the street, thus coinciding with the location of the cemetery as shown on Colonel José Sanchez-Navarro's map of the Alamo after the battle. After 1807 the mission cemetery was most likely sporadically used up until the battle of the Alamo. According to existing historical information, the remains of the Alamo defenders and the Mexican soldiers could be anywhere within a few thousand feet of the Alamo—in the form of cremated remains of the defenders, who may have been buried in a single area or several areas; or the remains of the defenders and/or Mexican attackers, which might be buried throughout the plaza area; or in the San Antonio River (where many of the bodies of the Mexican soldiers were hastily dumped after the battle). However, besides the battle "burial issue," there is the question of the burial of the earlier occupants of Mission San Antonio de Valero.

Headlines in an article by J. Carroll Markey in the Insight section of the Sunday *Express-News* dated August 1, 1982, read: "Alamo Burial Site Still A Mystery." A map of 1836 illustrates no less than six possible areas pinpointed as potential locations for the Alamo dead. The article discusses the inherent problems that have plagued researchers in locating the remains, one being exact historic accounts that provide accurate directional and areal indications. According to historical research and traditional accounts, the six possible burial sites include: an area east of the long barracks, a peach orchard in proximity to the Alamo, the old Santa Rosa Cemetery—at least for the remains of the dead soldiers of the Mexican army—the present-day location of St. Joseph's Catholic Church, and Juan Sequin's recollection that he gathered the burned remains of the defenders near the Menger Hotel.

Lt. Col. José Enrique de la Peña, shortly after the March 6, 1836 battle, recorded what he described as the burning of the bodies of the defenders in a large funeral pyre along with a majority of the 300 Mexican soldiers killed at the battle. It would appear that as the years rolled by after the famous battle, not only the location of the dead Alamo defenders changed, but so did the body count for those Mexican soldiers who perished in the battle. From 300 dead according to Peña, the figure rose to 500 plus when news reached Sam Houston and reached at least 1,500 within eighteen days after the battle—and the numbers continued to grow! The funeral pyre and burial locations for the defenders and Mexican soldiers continue to remain problematic and still spark controversy.

One account has 1,600 Mexican soldiers buried after the battle. Apparently, Francisco Antonio Ruiz, the alcalde of San Antonio, assisted in laying to rest in a cemetery south of the city on the Medina River many of the Mexican soldiers who died. When there was no more room for the dead, he ordered the remaining bodies to be thrown into the river (an unlikely scenario given the fact that honored dead are not usually so unceremoniously treated, but are given a Christian burial). Furthermore, Ruiz recalled helping to gather the bodies of the Texas defenders along with firewood from the nearby woods to construct a

81

funeral pyre, which was set ablaze later that evening. The location of the pyre and what happened to the remains after the fire was extinguished went unrecorded.

A physician named James Barnard, who visited San Antonio de Bexar a month after the Mexican army was defeated at San Jacinto, recalled visiting the spot where the funeral pyre was located. Covering the ground were the brittle, burned bones of the defenders lying among the ashes. His recollection placed the spot approximately 100 rods from the fort or chapel, but his failure to include a direction continued to fuel speculation as to where the bodies of the Alamo defenders were actually located.

Juan Sequin, according to his fading memory, some fifty years after the Alamo battle, collected the ashes of the defenders, which were in three piles, and placed them inside a casket. He then had the casket carried across the San Antonio River in full procession to the San Fernando parish church to be interred in graves that had been prepared to give them a Christian burial on February 25, 1837. The Alamo Association contacted Juan Seguin in 1889 when he was near death at the age of eighty-two. Seguin responded by saying that he had buried the remains in the San Fernando Cathedral even though a March 28, 1837 *Telegraph and Texas Register* article quoting the San Fernando clergy vehemently denied that Seguin had buried the remains of the Alamo defenders there. The truth behind Seguin's conflicting stories is still questioned by historians.

Although the precise location of the burial spot for the Alamo casualties was lost, a San Antonio visitor in 1843 named William Bollaert remembered viewing the burial area and described its location under peach trees a short distance from the Alamo. In 1848 a massive army cleanup of the Alamo Plaza area fronting the church supposedly encountered hastily covered bodies associated with fur caps and buckskin trapping—relics of the last stand, no doubt, if this story is true at all. In 1860 Captain Reuben Potter, who began his own personal research project, discussing the fall of the Alamo, described the burial site of the defenders as being a few hundred yards from the Alamo in what had once been a peach orchard but was now a vacant lot in the "Alamo suburb." Again, a key eyewitness failed to provide the exact location of the lot and its direction from the Alamo so as to be able to relocate the area. In 1878 other skeletal remains were unearthed in the chapel, but further investigation concluded that they belonged to the early mission period rather than the Alamo battle.

An 1882 Alamo City Guide proffered that the bodies of the Alamo defenders were taken to a location on Alameda Street near the present site of Saint Joseph's Catholic Church where a funeral pyre was constructed. Furthermore, the burned remains were then interred near the spot where the defenders gave their lives. A short time later, Mary Maverick, the president of the newly formed Alamo Monument Association, based on her recollections when she visited the area in 1838, believed that the ashes of the defenders had been buried between Blum and Crockett Streets or Blum and Houston Streets. Additionally, Maverick confirmed that the exact location of the burial area still remained a mystery.

In 1889 deputy county clerk Juan Barera recalled that in the 1840s, while a youngster, he often viewed a wooden monument which marked the spot where the remains of the Alamo defenders were buried—a spot located near the site of Saint Joseph's church. Judge Juan Rodriguez recalled Seguin bringing the remains together near or to the east of where the Menger Hotel now stands. He was adamant that it was highly unlikely the remains of the defenders would have been buried at the San Fernando church since Alcalde Ruiz was responsible for burying all the dead. Adina De Zavala suggested that tradition placed some of the defenders' remains in the courtyard east of the Alamo long barracks, while others were set ablaze on three funeral pyres to the south and southeast of the Alamo. In 1906 city clerk August Biesenback came forward with an account of the burials when he was in San Antonio as a child in 1858. He recalled watching the exhumation of the remains of the defenders from a long trench at 821 East Commerce Street and the reburial in the Odd Fellows Cemetery in the complex of old cemeteries on East Commerce. Charles Merritt Barnes found several witnesses who remembered the events of 1836 and concluded that the bodies of the defenders had been burned on two funeral pyres, one in the Ludlow yard and the other on the south side of the street approximately 250 yards to the east.

In 1920 human remains were again discovered on the corner of Alamo Plaza and Crockett Street, two hundred feet from the Alamo, at a depth of eighteen inches where a garage for Joseph Courand was being constructed. Prior to this, the area contained the Rotter Saloon at 302 Alamo Plaza, which, by 1919 had become Cowles Auto Livery. The saloon to livery structure was finally demolished for Courand's garage. The remains were thought to be either early Indian converts or remains of the Alamo defenders; however, the issue was never resolved. During a Works Progress Administration project in front of the chapel, workers unearthed about twenty fragments of what appeared to be burned human bone. Digging down three to four feet, the men discovered charred bones scattered through the earth. Again, they were believed to be the remains of either a fallen Alamo defender or an early settler: another unresolved discovery.

In 1935 more human remains were discovered within Alamo Plaza as a new post office was constructed to replace the old federal building. Evidently, a skull pierced by an arrowhead was unearthed outside what would have been the northeast corner of the plaza wall. Beads (probably from a rosary), a piece of pierced bone, a dish, and a copper ring were also recovered. The burials were believed to be associated with the mission period, and the materials were given to the superintendent of the San Fernando cemetery. The excavation continued as the new post office was being constructed, and additional burials (only skulls and larger bones) were found at a depth of approximately five feet. It was the opinion of some researchers that the remains were related to an epidemic, and they were buried outside the mission compound to prevent the spread of further disease. Others believed the burials were of Mexican soldiers cut down by the firepower of the Alamo sharpshooters. A Mexican woman contended that some of the Mexican soldiers, in a fit of remorse for mutilating the remains of the Alamo defenders, buried some of their bodies in the area of the post office.

Were these human remains from the mission period, the time of early settlement, the Alamo battle, or are they the bodies of Mexican soldiers? The truth may never be known.

During July 1936, throngs of clergy, public officials, and historians gathered to witness an excavation behind the altar of the San Fernando Cathedral. The apprehensive and excitable group concurred that the remains that were uncovered belonged to the Alamo heroes. Subsequently, in 1938 the relics were entombed in the church in a newly constructed mausoleum. Most historians discount the possibility that the relics belong to the Alamo defenders.

*Sarcophagus containing the reputed remains of the
Alamo heroes. Reverend Angel Conangla, a priest at the
San Fernando Mission, views the sarcophagus*
Photograph from The San Antonio Light Collection. Courtesy of The Institute of Texan Cultures

The year 1937 ushered in more discoveries of human remains: four burials, to be exact. Although the initial report indicated that they belonged to three adults and one child, the remains were sealed in a concrete, lead-lined vault and returned to their resting place before they could be professionally examined; a bronze marker in the floor of the chapel marks the site of the reburial. From the late 1930s to the present, questions still remain as to where almost 1,000 mission period remains are buried along with those on both sides who perished during the battle of the Alamo. The mystery remains, as do the reports of the spirits of Mission San Antonio de Valero—the Alamo!

A Gateway to Another World

Santa Anna gave the orders to burn the Texan dead. Old records indicate there were two, possibly three funeral pyres prepared, and the bodies were stacked "like cordwood" to smolder for days. Denied the dignity of a Christian burial, killed in sudden and violent action, it is no wonder that even today there are many accounts of "strange things . . . noises . . .cold spots" associated with the Alamo and the long barracks museum where the fiercest of the fighting is reported to have taken place.

Williams and Byrne, *Spirits of San Antonio and South Texas* (1993)

It is no wonder then, with this kind of legacy, that strange and unexplainable events continue to occur within a limestone frame containing so many memories.

The remnant energy of Mission de Valero can be seen, heard, and felt. For those who have come into contact with the spiritual side of this icon of freedom, the mysteries surrounding the hallowed grounds are all too real. Perhaps this spot, like so many cemeteries and battlefields, belongs to a "dead zone" where past and present confront each other as co-existing dimensions.

The Alamo circa 1890
Hugo and Schemeltzer's store is adjacent to the north.
Photograph from *The San Antonio Express-News*.
Courtesy of The Institute of Texan Cultures, San Antonio

As some parapsychologists suggest, where so much emotional energy has been concentrated, there is bound to be a residual force of psychic scars and, therefore, a potential for hauntings. With this book, one can take a guided or self-guided tour around the remains of the energy-filled and hallowed Alamo grounds. You can become a part of a special journey into the unknown and, "if the spirit is willing," you might be given a firsthand opportunity to experience the supernatural.

Although skeptics attribute the multitude of unexplained phenomena to events and circumstances that science can explain or simply to overactive imaginations, there are those who have had experiences which defy logic and cannot be summarily dismissed. Make no mistake; a number of people, believers and skeptics alike, with no reason to manufacture the truth, have witnessed the paranormal at the Alamo. These people have no illusion about what they experienced. They have become believers in the fact that something from another dimension crossed their paths—but why?

A Question of Belief

Of all the uncertainties that exist, death, ghosts, and the afterlife remain the most mysterious and intriguing. The concept defies logic, eludes scientific explanation, and escapes absolute proof yet is an integral part of our belief system. It has become an obsession for many to prove as well as disprove the concept of life after death. There has always been a deep regard and fascination for the subject that will continue long after we have left this physical plane.

Wlodarski, Wlodarski, and Senate,
A Guide to the Haunted Queen Mary (1995)

The age-old question remains: Do we survive death? If so, why do some choose to remain here? Does the spirit or some form of energy remain locked in time and space? Does it remain, out of choice, to fulfill a specific purpose? Does a ghost represent a remnant of energy from an unresolved tragedy, a residue from an event that continues to repeat itself, waiting for justice or resolution and a way to end the cycle? Are they unhappy souls looking for help, messengers or angels from another level trying to help us overcome our fear of death or save us from an impending tragedy, or do they willingly remain in a given space because of pleasant memories, returning to a particular place at a point in their lives when they were happy and at peace?

L.B. Taylor, in his book *The Ghosts of Virginia* (1995: xi-xiv), suggests that there are a number of commonly offered explanations for why ghosts exist. They may represent a surviving emotional memory of someone who died but is unaware of his/her passing. They are generally spontaneous apparitions that suggest the real presence of someone distant or dead. Ghosts represent the spirit of a deceased individual who still actually inhabits some other sphere of existence and is occasionally able to manifest itself to certain people in this physical plane. They are manifestations of assorted unconscious wishes, unresolved guilt, or patchwork imaginings. Ghosts represent a disembodied spirit or energy, which manifests itself over a long period of time in one location. They are consistent with the known characteristics of someone who has died in a specific place, with the deceased's personality sill active and functioning. Ghosts can be observed, heard, smelled, felt, or known to be present by our "sixth sense." They are manifestations of persistent personal energy as an indication that some kind of force survives death and is being exorcised after death, which in some way is connected with a person previously known on earth. Ghosts are illusions created by a powerful class of beings who appear as dead human beings to contact, help, or hurt the living. Ghosts are images, somehow recorded on a sensitive medium and visible under certain conditions to people in a particular state of mind, similar to an instant replay. A ghost is the soul, which leaves the body at death but, under certain circumstances, remains behind rather than proceeding to the "other side." They represent telepathic messages from their lingering bodiless minds rather than souls of the dead. They are simply souls stuck in this dimension, repeating old habits or lingering because of unresolved circumstances such as unrequited love or unresolved tragedy. They were associated with a particular house all or most of their lives and feel it still belongs to them, and current tenants may be thought of as intruders. Ghosts return to search for a lost lover; they come back to complete some unfinished business in life. They sometimes reenact activities or events of the past, perhaps bound to their haunting ground by a powerful emotion or event that prevents them from passing completely to the "other side"; or they return to atone for some perceived or real mistake they committed while living.

If wars and conflicts leave energy scars or psychic imprints on the visible landscape (many battlefields appear to be haunted by recurring scenes of bloody encounters and traumatic events), then the Alamo qualifies as a location where deep psychic scars and residual energy are still attached. First built as Mission San Antonio de Valero, the remaining buildings are associated with arguably the most important event in Texas history—the Battle of the Alamo. After a thirteen-day period in February and March of 1836, all the brave defenders of the Alamo, outnumbered over twenty to one, died on March 6. The defense of this outpost cost the lives of over 180 Texians, as they were known, while over one thousand Mexican soldiers under the command of General Lopez Antonio de Santa Anna also perished.

The defenders of the Alamo, however, are not the only ones who apparently haunt Mission San Antonio de Valero. Before one of the defining moments in Texas history unfolded, the area was the scene of other calamities. After the founding of the mission, attacks by the Native American inhabitants continued for many years. Death came to the Native Americans, the Spanish missionaries, and those who became converts as well as the early settlers of the mission and Villa de Bexar. The harsh reality of frontier existence took its toll on several thousand people prior to the carnage inflicted at the Battle of the Alamo. Death by Indian attack, disease, personal tragedy, imprudent confrontations, and severe lifestyle all left imprints on the landscape—and these untimely deaths create the potential for hauntings.

It is no wonder, then, that in addition to those who died establishing the mission, psychic imprints of the defenders of the Alamo and the Mexican soldiers who fought for what they believed in are sometimes picked up by more "sensitive" individuals in and around the Alamo. Stepping inside what remains of the Alamo is like stepping back in time. It has a feeling and energy all its own, an emotional charge that many may be fortunate enough to experience.

The Alamo—A Haunted Beginning

There is something marvelous beyond the horizon of death and the limit of our sight. It becomes personal knowledge when our minds are coaxed out of the shadows of the purely material world and into the brilliance and brightness of the world of the spirit that lies just beyond the limit of our sight.

H.P. Lovecraft

The following story was excerpted from *Spirits of San Antonio and South Texas* by Docia Schultz Williams and Renata Byrne (1993). Permission was granted by Wordware Publishing, Inc., Plano, Texas.

The death of the insurgent Alamo defenders was not enough for the disgruntled commander, Santa Anna. Instead of providing a Christian burial for these rebel defenders who dared to defy the Napoleon of the West, he had their lifeless corpses dragged to funeral pyres and burned. One suggested location was on old "Alameda," (821 East Commerce Street, just east of present-day St. Joseph's Catholic Church). A second area may have been located where Brentanos bookstore is located today on the lower level of the Rivercenter Mall. A third location may have been where the fire station was constructed east of the Alamo on Houston Street.

As for Santa Anna's men, many were hurriedly buried in shallow graves near the Alamo or thrown into a well that has, to this day, eluded archaeologists. Some bodies were even dumped in the nearby San Antonio River and slowly carried out to sea. According to witnesses who were children at the time of the fall of the Alamo, the bodies were stacked "like cordwood" on funeral pyres, with the stench of the smoke filling the air for days.

The Alamo circa 1900
Photograph from *The San Antonio Express-News*
Courtesy of The Institute of Texan Cultures, San Antonio

Denied the dignity of a Christian burial and killed suddenly and violently, it is no wonder that there are many accounts of "strange things . . . noises . . . cold spots" associated with the Alamo and the long barracks where the fiercest of the fighting is reported to have occurred. It didn't take long after the fall of the Alamo for ghosts to be spotted. According to numerous historical accounts, after surrendering to Sam Houston at the battle of San Jacinto, Santa Anna ordered a small Mexican force still in San Antonio under General Andrade to destroy the Alamo. As Andrade moved his small force out of the city, he left the destruction of the fortress to his subordinate Colonel

94

Sanchez. Sanchez left with a few men to fulfill his orders when they witnessed a most unusual event. The men quickly returned with a look of horror on their faces and stories of phantasms. Much to the chagrin of General Andrade, not only was the Alamo still intact, but it was apparently guarded by evil spirits according to the frightened remnant of the army. The chapel remained intact despite the efforts of the Mexicans to destroy all traces of what Santa Anna feared might one day become a shrine rather than a chapter in his history of conquest.

Sanchez and his men refused to return to the Alamo. They claimed they had been visited by six ghostly forms—standing in a semicircle holding swords of fire—who blocked their entry to the building! The soldiers swore they saw figures they described as "diablos" (devils). An angry Andrade, fearless when it came to dealing with battling the living, decided to visit the place himself and put an end to the rumors of evil spirits and devils. Apparently, Andrade reached the remains of the Alamo and witnessed, firsthand, the ghostly protectors of the mission. The chapel was thus spared as the general hastened a quick retreat from the town he had held for Mexico since March 6. Whoever the spirits were, Mexican, Texian, or both, one thing was certain: They did not want the chapel destroyed, not after they had fought so hard and died so valiantly in the great battle. It seems that, for once, the spirits of both sides were finally able to join in the same cause.

During 1871 the City of San Antonio demolished the last remaining portions of the original mission, except for the chapel and long barracks, which contained two rooms on either side of the main gate on the south wall. However, this event apparently did not meet with the approval of the ghostly dwellers of the fortress. According to the accounts of guests staying at the nearby Menger Hotel, several people watched in astonishment and disbelief as spectral forms marched along the walls of the rooms!

Another incident is documented in the *San Antonio Express News* on February 5, 1894, when the city used the Alamo property as a headquarters for the police. A newspaper story read, "The Alamo is again the center of interest to quite a number of curious people who have been attracted by the rumors of the manifestations of alleged ghosts. They are said to be holding bivouac around that place so sacred to the memory of Texas's historic dead. There is nothing new about the stories told. There is the same measured tread of the ghostly sentry as he crosses the south side of the roof from east to west, the same tale of buried treasure, and the same manifestations of fear by the American citizen of African descent as he passes and repasses the historic ground. The only variation appears to be in the fact that the sound of feet on the roof has been heard as late as five o'clock in the morning by the officer in charge who says that the sounds are never heard except on rainy or drizzly nights. He attributes the whole matter to some cause growing out of the condition of the roof during rainy weather but could not give any reason why the same causes that produced the sounds at night did not produce similar sounds in daylight hours."

The newspaper article continued its story with the arrival of Leon Mareschal and his fourteen-year-old daughter, Mary, who came to the police headquarters one Saturday night. Introducing themselves to Captain Jacob Coy, who was on duty, they claimed they could communicate with the ghosts of the Alamo. An amused Coy gave his guests two chairs, and the three of them adjourned to the little-used jail room adjoining the station office. Mareschal's daughter was placed in a trance, and Coy was told to ask her questions. The bemused captain in charge of the Alamo, without mincing words, asked the girl if she saw spirits in the chapel. The young girl replied in a faint voice that there were men here. Coy then instructed the girl to tell the spirits to form a line and state their names. The young girl twitched her head from side to side and responded that the ghostly legion had fallen in line and that they were the spirits of the Alamo.

Alamo Plaza circa 1912-1913
North side of Alamo Plaza with post office to the left
and ruins of the long barracks on the right.
Courtesy of The Institute of Texan Cultures, San Antonio

The answer was too vague to suit Coy, so he continued by asking why they visited the place and caused all the noise in the building at night. The girl indicated that the spirits were anxiously looking for a treasure buried within the walls of the Alamo, a tidy sum of $540,000 in twenty-dollar gold pieces. Furthermore, they were anxious for the money to be discovered and would relinquish all claims to the treasure to the person who found it. A curious Coy then asked where it was buried. Without hesitation, the girl, without looking, pointed toward a dingy little apartment in the southwest corner of the Alamo. Shortly after that, about one o'clock in the morning, Mareschal and his daughter got up and disappeared into the night. No reference has been found to substantiate or refute the claim of buried gold within the confines of the Alamo.

Reports continued to circulate about guards and watchmen, who were supposed to patrol the inner sanctum of the building late at night, refusing to do so because of unexplainable sounds and the feeling of "presences." In August 1897 another article told of tourists who, after visiting the Alamo, talked about ghosts and mysterious shadows in the gloomy recesses in the rear of the building. Others have heard moaning sounds, hissing whispers, and the clanking of chains on stormy nights. Some believe that not all the eerie sounds are those of the defenders of the Alamo or their attackers. One theory has it that ghosts of the Franciscan monks also haunt the mission, religious apparitions of those who occupied the buildings prior to it being used as a fort. They were believed to represent repentant monks who broke their vows and were punished for their violations by being manacled in the dark confines of the building.

Over the years, ghosts, apparitions, and paranormal events have not only been witnessed by those whose job it was to work at the Alamo, but by visitors and spiritualists, mediums, and ghost hunters who have devoted their lives to researching the paranormal. The resounding answer is that something lurks within the walls of the fortress. One local psychic was rumored to have become tuned into the energy there even before setting foot within its walls. He saw a lesser-known defender still inhabiting the fortress attending to wounded soldiers. The psychic confirmed that, oddly enough, many of the spirits or entities were those of Santa Anna's army who died in combat, still lingering near the place where they fought bravely for their own cause. Some of these soldiers came over to convince the defenders to surrender and were murdered by their own men for an act of treason. The psychic confirmed a long-believed notion that the souls of so many remained near the Alamo because they were not given a Christian burial. Their deaths were so violent and their lives ended so abruptly that their souls appear to be caught in a kind of "limbo" at the shrine.

Williams and Byrne (1993:10) concluded, "The Alamo doesn't seem threatening or frightening to us. It pulls at our heartstrings when we enter. We are filled with reverence and respect when we enter into this shrine to freedom. Under the gentle custodianship of the Daughters of the Republic of Texas, the Alamo has fallen into tender, loving hands. The dignity of those who died defending it is well preserved, and the turbulence of its past now rests in the pages of history. Our fervent hope is that the spirits of those brave defenders have at last found their eternal peace."

An Overwhelming Feeling at the Alamo

I am thy father's spirit, Doom'd for a certain term to walk the night. And for the day confin'd to fast in fires, Till the foul crimes done in my days of nature are burnt and purg'd way. But that I am forbid to tell the secrets of my prison-house, I could a tale unfold whose lightest word would harrow up thy soul, freeze thy young blood, make thy two eyes like stars start from their spheres, and each particular hair to stand on end, like quills upon the fearful porpentine.

From Shakespeare's Ode to the Ghost of Hamlet's Father

J.M. of Green Bay, Wisconsin, conveys a feeling that many Alamo visitors have experienced. In the 1940s, while J.M. was in the military and stationed in San Antonio, he toured the monument for the first time on a daytime pass. Upon entering the chapel, he was immediately overcome with great sorrow such as he had never experienced before. He attributed this to the tragic history of the Alamo; however, he never had a similar feeling in any other place he had visited. In the 1950s, J.M. once again visited San Antonio while on a trip to show his two young sons where he had been stationed in the military. They also decided to visit the Alamo since they had never been there. When he entered the building, J.M. again experienced a similar feeling of melancholy as had overwhelmed him ten years earlier. Finally, a few years later, he attended a convention with his wife in San Antonio. She wanted to visit the Alamo, so they both stopped over to see the shrine. For a third time, J.M., entered the chapel where he was once again overcome with a feeling of loss and heartbreak; this time, the sensation was so strong that he told his wife he had to leave immediately.

Since then, J.M. has made his way back to the Alamo twice, with the same feeling recurring upon each visit. During his last trip, the feeling was so powerful that J.M. broke down and cried openly from a feeling of depression, which followed him into the courtyard. He has no knowledge of past lives or psychic abilities, but the Alamo is the only place in the world that affects him like that. Even when he "lost very close family members or friends, (he) never experienced that kind of sadness and grief."

The Alamo circa 1930
Interior of the Alamo chapel.
Photograph from *The San Antonio Express-News*
Courtesy of The Institute of Texan Cultures, San Antonio

101

The Duke Remembers the Alamo

I think that some people want me to explain why the apparitions have occurred, and continue to occur and why seemingly unexplainable and illogical visions pop up out of nowhere and just as suddenly and inexplicably return to wherever it was they came from. I cannot fully explain it. Some people look toward the existence of ghosts as a sort of proof, a validation that there is another life after this one, that death is not the final Victor, but merely the Great Imposter.

Mark Nesbitt, *More Ghosts of Gettysburg* (1992)

John Wayne was born Marion Michael Morrison in 1907 in Winterset, Iowa. A legendary star, his Hollywood career spanned over forty years. In the late 1950s Wayne decided to direct a movie that embodied his philosophy. Prior to directing the movie *The Alamo* in Brackettville, a few miles from San Antonio and the "real " Alamo, Wayne resolved to make his movie as historically accurate as possible, so he extensively researched the historical backdrop to the battle. He was also determined not to create a false-front film set; rather, he spent over $1.5 million re-creating the Alamo and, with his production designer and set designer, set out to make an exact replica of the original structure.

He consulted the actual blueprints as well as documents relating to the sequence of events that led to the fall of the Alamo on March 6, 1836. In a bigger-than-life spectacle, Wayne, as director, and his talented technical advisors, crew, all-star cast, which included Richard Widmark, Laurence Harvey, Chill Wills, Frankie Avalon,

Patrick Wayne, Linda Crystal, and Richard Boone, and extras re-enacted the famous battle for Texas Independence. Because of the success of the movie, the replica set of the Alamo became a highly regarded and much-visited tourist attraction. According to some individuals, Wayne gave so much of himself in making the epic movie that he may have left a little of himself behind—as a ghostly visitor at the "real" Alamo.

From B.C. of San Antonio comes a story pertaining to the legend of John Wayne. According to B.C., John Wayne, while filming *The Alamo*, became obsessed with the area, the history of the battle, and its heroic defenders. His obsession drove him to spend a fortune on re-creating the Alamo for the purpose of historical accuracy. It is rumored that, after his death, his spirit was seen at the Alamo, apparently visiting and talking with the fallen defenders, a journey he still takes today although his ghost is seen infrequently. Furthermore, B.C. recalls that a psychic was brought in to confirm the story, and she apparently communicated with some of the spirits who remain within the Alamo. The psychic, through her spirit contacts, said that Wayne visits the Alamo about once a month. There was no answer forthcoming as to his whereabouts between visits to the Alamo.

In an article in the Sunday edition of the *San Antonio Express News* dated January 27, 1991, Charles Long, the former curator of the Alamo museum, recalled taking John Wayne on a tour of the historic mission when Wayne was filming his epic movie *The Alamo*. Pilar, Wayne's widow, wrote in his biography that the story of the Alamo was the epitome of everything Wayne stood for—stamina, courage, and patriotism; therefore, it would not surprise her if his spirit visits the place where so many brave men gave their lives for such a noble cause.

The article continued by saying that San Antonio psychic Joe Holbrook was called upon to see what he could "pick up on" inside the Alamo. Agreeing to visit the sacred landmark with newspaper reporter Craig Phelon, Holbrook, while driving in his car, reportedly began communicating with the spirits of the Texian defenders and sensing images of the battle before reaching the landmark. He was able to focus on one defender in particular. He identified himself to Holbrook as a bootmaker and defender named Morgan, with the nickname "Boots." He was responsible for tending to the Alamo wounded.

The Alamo circa 1939
Overview of the Alamo and compound area.
Photograph from *The San Antonio Express-News*
Courtesy of The Institute of Texan Cultures, San Antonio

Holbrook related certain information to Phelon regarding the trapped Alamo spirits by saying, "They don't just linger around the same place all the time." Holbrook felt that in any place where people have died, there are usually spirit sightings from time to time. Upon entering the chapel, Holbrook picked up so much energy that it was hard for him to focus; however, he was drawn to the room just left of the main entrance, stating, "There are six of them right in here." The irony, according to Holbrook, was that the spirits were not of the Alamo defenders but belonged instead to Santa Anna's men and were still wearing their Mexican army uniforms.

To Phelon's amazement, Holbrook came up with the names of three spirits, including two brothers named Raul and Pablo Fuentes; they were seventeen and eighteen years old when they were killed during the battle according to Holbrook. The third belonged to a lieutenant named Pedro Escalante who "told" Holbrook that the brothers crossed the line to help the defenders because they wanted the defenders to surrender and stop fighting—a decision that cost them their lives. A final communication from the dead via the psychic confirmed that Wayne does come back to visit the fortress and those who bravely defended it. Apparently, John Wayne's passion for the Alamo continued beyond the grave and into the afterlife!

No Logical Explanation

The white men will never be alone. These shores will swarm with the invisible dead. The dead are not powerless. Dead, did I say? There is no death, only a change of worlds.

An anonymous Native American chief

R.D. of Texas relates two tales from the supernatural based on actual events that occurred while he worked as a ranger at the Alamo—events for which he can offer no logical explanation. R.D. makes no claim to have seen a "ghost" or heard "spirits." As a twenty-year law enforcement veteran, he has been taught that everything has an explanation (a philosophy he wholeheartedly embraces); however, for these events, he could offer no reassuring answers.

While working with the Alamo rangers from 1988 through 1991, two incidents occurred. The first took place while R.D. was on duty after the Alamo closed, around 5:00 P.M. It was in the winter and as his job required, R.D. made his usual inspection of the grounds in search of tourists still wandering around. As he made his rounds, he patrolled the long barracks. Walking alone through the north end of the barracks, he had already locked and closed the south end. As he was about to exit and lock the door, he began hearing voices. At first the voices were barely audible; however, they became louder by the second. It was more of a murmur. Thinking perhaps the strange whisper might belong to a custodian in the building, R.D. began walking back through toward the south end of the building but found no one.

The murmuring continued growing louder as he approached the south end, yet R.D. could not clearly understand any distinct words—that is, until he returned to the north end of the long barracks on his way to exit the building. Only then was he able to clearly hear a voice call out, "It's too late." R.D. did not wait around to ask what it was "too late" for. He immediately exited and secured the building as quickly as he could. Upon returning to the ranger office in the rear of the grounds, he related the incident to his chief. The chief didn't think that R.D. was crazy; he merely smiled and, with a knowing look, began relating an incident that happened to him while working at the Alamo.

The Alamo in 1936
Photograph of the Alamo and its arched hallway
Courtesy of The Institute of Texan Cultures, San Antonio

107

What R.D had heard was not unusual, according to the chief, but another in a long line of stories focusing on unexplainable events, which continued to occur on the Alamo grounds. On a historical note, at the time of the battle for the Alamo, the long barracks was part of the courtyard complex that was connected to the chapel by a twelve-foot wall that ran west for 50 feet from the northwest corner of the chapel. The barracks, a two-story structure, 186 feet long by 18 feet wide and 18 feet high, served as the hospital and supported a light gun and artillerymen on top. From the roof, they defended the plaza, courtyard, and palisade next to the chapel during the final siege. Some historians and survivor Susanna Dickinson place Davy Crockett's last stand next to the long barracks in front of the chapel. Perhaps the voices and words, "It's too late," R.D. heard that night in the long barracks belonged to the defenders, confirming the worst—that Santa Anna's men were at their doorstep about to kill all the brave defenders.

R.D had another encounter with the unknown. One lonely winter night, while on patrol after leaving the main office at around midnight, he was startled to see the figure of a man walking behind the chapel. The man appeared to be wearing a long coat and a tall hat and was walking with his head down. Still over forty yards away and thinking this might be a trespasser, R.D. called out for the man to stop. The figure turned and appeared to look directly at him; however, R.D. still couldn't make out many details or distinctive features other than the person sported a large, bushy moustache.

As R.D. moved closer, the figure turned and walked toward the gift shop, passing between a small tree and the rear of the chapel, and disappeared out of R.D.'s range of vision. He waited a few seconds for the strange visitor to emerge from behind the tree. When the man failed to materialize, as if he had simply vanished, R.D gave pursuit. He conducted a thorough search of the area and found to his dismay that whoever or whatever it was could not be found. The gentleman in a long coat and top hat who sported a moustache may have stepped out of time to briefly visit his old haunting ground, remaining just long enough for R.D. to glimpse the past in the present.

On more than one occasion, R.D. opened the chapel in the morning and noticed Davy Crockett's portrait hanging askew. It is up too high (ten feet above the floor) for anyone to reach—at least with human legs.

The Alamo pre-1945
Photograph from *The San Antonio Express-News*
Courtesy of The Institute of Texan Cultures, San Antonio

109

I'm Not An Alarmist, But!..

A ghost is the soul which survives the body. Sometimes it is wrapped in an earth covering which makes it heavy and visible, and drags it down to the visible region.

Plato

Former Alamo ranger and present-day amateur historian W.M. was willing to share what he had encountered while working at the Alamo. He qualified the information by stating quite emphatically that he is not an alarmist or a believer in the paranormal; however, his personal experiences, while with Alamo security, defy logic and explanation.

The first story concerns itself with a generally known and often-repeated phenomenon among rangers that occurs in the Alamo gift shop: the appearance of a little boy in one of the high interior windows. W.M. is one of several rangers along with a handful of visitors to see the strange presence staring down from a deserted window overlooking the courtyard area. There is no physical way for a child, even if he were to sneak into the building, to be able to climb that high; besides, there's nothing he could use to stand on.

According to legend, the little boy may have been a small child who was evacuated from the Alamo during the last days of the siege in 1836. Perhaps, his father, brother, or uncle stayed behind to defend the fortress, and the boy remains behind in a kind of netherworld continuing to look for the relative. Even though the gift shop was not there at the time of the battle (having been constructed in the 1930s), it may be a location where he last recalls seeing his relative alive. Whatever the reason for the child's appearance, according to eyewitnesses, he usually appears around the same time every year during the first weeks of February staring sadly out from a window of the gift shop. The descriptions are alike in that the image is one of a young child between ten and twelve years old with blonde hair, who stares out of the high windows of the gift shop at those who watch in amazement below. Furthermore, security checks after each report revealed that no one was inside. Given the window height above ground level plus the fact that there is no ledge inside the building to support a person and no other way to climb up, the mystery only deepens. The fact remains that a young boy continues to return to the gift shop and is only visible above the waist, never as a complete figure, and he seems content to peer out the window at those curious and bold enough to return the stare.

Another story by W.M. involves the sighting of the figure of a man wearing frontier, buckskin clothing and carrying a long rifle on the Alamo grounds. The figure has been spotted on a number of occasions at various times of the year in the rear of the chapel near the northeast corner. He appears to be standing upright and holding onto a flintlock rifle. He is standing at attention. Some individuals have spotted the ghostly soldier wearing a buckskin shirt, pants, moccasins, and a coonskin cap from different angles, which rules out the possibility that it may be an optical illusion related to shadows cast by the cactus surrounding the chapel or to the cactus itself. The first thought that comes to mind from those who have been fortunate to spot the specter is that it may be the ghost of Davy Crockett. If it is, perhaps Davy is still keeping a keen eye out for Mexican attackers while clinging to his favorite rifle.

W.M. experienced three more eerie encounters with the unknown within the confines of the Alamo grounds. The first occurred at night. While performing his standard patrol of the grounds long after the Alamo was closed to the public, he heard the distinct sound of the back door to the chapel being shut. As a matter of procedure and part of the regular inspection performed by the Alamo rangers, all doors and windows are routinely secured after the Alamo closes. W.M. had personally turned off all the lights, shut off all the power, and performed all the designated tasks prior to this intrusion. The sound of a door being opened or closed usually meant that someone was there without permission. In this case, he also considered the possibility of the powerful air conditioning unit inside the chapel creating the sound of pressure on the door. He quickly walked over to where the sound emanated and began an inspection of the interior of the chapel.

The Alamo circa 1935
During the installation of flagstone paving for the entrance walkway
Photograph from The San Antonio Light Collection.
Courtesy of The Institute of Texan Cultures, San Antonio

112

Upon entering and after the doors swung shut, W.M. got the shock of his life. Standing off to his right was a buckskin-clad man leaning against one of the viewing boxes. He knew instantly that this was not a tourist or any ordinary person. W.M. was frozen in his tracks for a few beats as he observed the man, whom he remembered as being around five feet tall, his head barely reaching above the level of the case, just standing there in silence. After gaining his composure, W.M. approached the man, who, at that point, simply vanished into thin air! He couldn't believe what he had just witnessed, but a careful inspection of the premises confirmed what his eyes had just shown him. There was no one else inside the deserted chapel. Perhaps the man from the past just came to observe the displays and look at his own history.

Another encounter took place in the long barracks, a place where paranormal sightings are common. While making another of his usual inspections and patrolling along the east side of the long barracks, W.M. checked the doors to make sure they were locked and that no one had managed to sneak in since he last inspected the area. It was then that he heard the distinct sound of footsteps (almost as if someone was walking around with boots on) coming from inside the barracks. He advised security by radio of a possible intruder. Their sensitive listening devices were attuned to hear the slightest disturbance from within and confirmed that "someone" was inside making noise besides W.M. He went in to inspect the premises with some apprehension. There wasn't a ranger who was ever certain what to expect when patrolling the Alamo grounds late at night—unexplainable things were usually occurring. With this in mind, W.M. remained cautious as he entered the long barracks through the door to the theater.

As W.M. entered, he noted nothing visually. As part of a routine to search for people who try to spend the night without permission, he walked through each room in the barracks, moving from the south end of the building to the north. Proceeding toward the northerly rooms, he began experiencing the sensation of something extremely cold pressing against his face and heard the distinct sound of footsteps following behind him. Not to be deterred, he slowly and cautiously proceeded from room to room, looking in all directions and expecting to spot his intruder at any moment. The sound of the footsteps following behind him was confirmed by security, which also heard the distinct sounds of not only one but two sets of footsteps on the monitoring equipment. By this time, W.M. was anxious to leave the building and, after a thorough inspection, did so without finding out to whom the footsteps belonged. If there was an intruder, he had managed to become invisible. The event became one in a long series of unexplainable occurrences in the long barracks.

A final encounter with the bizarre and unusual occurred one night while W.M. was standing in the grassy area in front of the chapel. As he gazed at the entrance, something caught his eye. To his amazement, a figure appeared in the window above the front door. The person was clearly visible inside the chapel window nonchalantly looking down at Alamo Plaza. Given the facts that it was long past closing and a person was standing in a window where few people had access, even during normal working hours, added to the strange feeling that passed through W.M.. For a few heartbeats, he could only watch in disbelief at the "visitor" in the chapel window. An approaching tourist jolted him back to reality. As they began to converse, W.M. chanced to look up at the window again, but the figure was gone.

The Alamo circa 1935
Overview of the Alamo following beautification work done in the mid-1930s
From The San Antonio Express-News. Courtesy of The Institute of Texan Cultures, San Antonio

Adding to W.M.'s astonishment, the tourist asked if he had ever seen a face in the chapel window. Before W.M. could respond, the visitor told him that he and his friends had a picture of a man standing inside the chapel window! They subsequently sent it to W.M. The image projecting from the Alamo chapel window could not be explained. Perhaps he was a defender or someone from the time when the Alamo functioned as a mission. Whoever or whatever it is still appears in the chapel window to those who happen to be in the right spot at the right time.

115

A Long Barracks Night

Then a spirit passed before my face; the hair on my flesh stood up.

The Book of Job

Several former Alamo rangers, as well as a handful of workmen, have had their share of strange encounters with the unknown in or near the long barracks. One former ranger elaborated on a particular event that took place one evening.

Patrolling the Alamo grounds during the early years used to be a solitary assignment with a lone ranger responsible for maintaining the security of the grounds. Prior to the implementation of a single-key system, which would essentially lock and unlock all the doors to existing structures, a guard was saddled with a dozen or more keys to open individual buildings while making his rounds. On one memorable occasion, the ranger was routinely inspecting the long barracks and was in the process of locking up when he had a brush with the paranormal. As was customary in terms of procedures, the ranger entered the long barracks through the middle door to inspect for intruders or pranksters. He opened the door and stepped inside the barracks. Upon entering, he locked the door behind him, securing the room. With a flashlight in hand, the unsuspecting ranger proceeded north toward a series of adjoining rooms.

116

The Alamo, 1936
From Bartlette Cocke Sr., San Antonio, Texas
Courtesy of The Institute of Texan Cultures, San Antonio

Just as the ranger was about to enter the next room and only a few dozen steps from the door he had just entered and secured, he heard what appeared to be the distinct sound of the door opening and slamming shut. The ranger was startled because he was positive that no one else could have been in there with him. He had inspected all the exterior doors, and there was only one set of keys, which were passed from one ranger to the other upon completion of each shift. He hurried back to the area where he heard the door close; it was still locked.

Thinking that someone had broken in and somehow forced his way out of the building, the ranger gave chase and immediately exited the building to complete a search of the adjoining grounds. He reasoned that, surely, if someone had just left the building a moment earlier, he would catch sight of the person hurrying away. Such was not the case, however; a thorough inspection of the grounds revealed nothing.

With the event fresh in the ranger's mind, yet with a job still to complete, he re-entered the long barracks, searched every room, but found nothing. The ranger became yet another in a long line of those who had become unwilling participants in the strange events that were associated with the long barracks.

I Was Not Overly Interested in Ghosts...

Ghost stories, landscape legends, and calendar customs can be seen as multi-layered experiences and events informing us about the past from a different viewpoint and heightening awareness of ourselves and the world in which we live. Even a 'simple' ghost story can tell us about the physical history of a landscape, the origins of a particular house and family, the psychology and sociology of the people who saw the ghost, and how it was reported in the media. As always, the mystery of the unknown remains to tantalize us, to hint that the universe may be, in the words of one famous physicist, "not only stranger than we imagine but stranger than we can imagine."

Andy Roberts, *Ghosts and Legends of Yorkshire* (1992)

Former Alamo ranger M.L. came forward with more stories regarding unexplainable events that took place while he worked at the Alamo on two different occasions between 1977 and 1979 and again between 1988 and 1989.

When M.L. was first employed at the Alamo, the individual buildings were not yet security alarmed as they are today. Before the new security system was functioning, a single ranger was responsible for securing the Alamo grounds, closing the gates, and making a final inspection to ensure that the interior of each building was locked and that no intruders were hiding inside. M.L. was not very familiar with the historical details of the 1836 Alamo battle when he first arrived as a ranger; however, as time

119

The Alamo circa 1936
Aerial photograph of the Alamo.
From *The San Antonio Express-News.*
Courtesy of The Institute of Texan Cultures, San Antonio

went on, he not only learned the history but received a number of firsthand history lessons from other-worldly teachers.

Reiterating that he is not a person who is or was overly interested in the subject of ghosts, unexplainable voices, or other similar phenomena, M.L.'s opinion changed somewhat over the years he was employed as an Alamo ranger. His initial encounter with the "spirits of the Alamo" occurred sometime during January or February 1978. He remembers the weather being cold and dreary as he was working the 4:30 P.M. to 12:30 A.M. shift. Always working alone on his shift while patrolling the grounds,

M.L. recalls checking the long barracks as part of his routine duties as a guard. Before entering the barracks, he distinctly heard what seemed like several voices coming from inside the building. Given the time and the fact that the building was locked and the security system activated, the voices were certainly unexpected. Unafraid and determined to find the source of the loud noise, M.L. entered the long barracks.

Upon entering, M.L. instantly noted that the voices which were readily apparent from the outside the structure were almost hushed once he stepped inside. Additionally, the noises appeared to be coming from the rear or northernmost area of the building. As he proceeded toward what he thought was the source of the eerie voices, the noise seemed to greatly diminish, and its location shifted to the area he had just come from. At first he only made out faint mumbling; however, as he continued to walk the barracks, words became clearer. They were not complete sentences, only quick responses. He found himself listening to a staccato of brief injunctions including: "No! Stop! Here they come! Fire! Dead!" M.L. was never able to locate the people who spoke these words, but after a thorough search of the building, he left assured that no one from the earthly plane had uttered them.

On another occasion, sometime during February or March 1978, M.L. recalled hearing "voices" and in particular, that of a woman crying while he secured the chapel.

This happened on several occasions to M.L., and each time he was unable to locate the source. On a particularly cold San Antonio night in late February or early March, about 11:00 to 11:30 P.M., while sitting in the security office, M.L. noticed that the moon was extremely bright (at that time, the security office was located in what was known as the "Old Greenhouse"). As M.L. peered out toward the chapel in the moonlight, he was awe-struck to

121

The Alamo circa 1937
Restoration work on the Alamo. View from the roof of the Crockett Hotel
Photograph from The San Antonio Light Collection
Courtesy of The Institute of Texan Cultures, San Antonio

see two men emerge from what appeared to be the rear wall of the chapel and walk toward the acequia. As he watched in disbelief, the two men reached the acequia, then changed directions and sauntered over to an eighteen-pound cannon, which was situated on the bridge over the acequia.

Assuming that people had managed to slip into the Alamo grounds, M.L. immediately jumped from his chair and rushed out of the office in hot pursuit of the two men. Trespassing was common in those days as people would climb the walls enclosing the Alamo in an attempt to have their own, private, after-hours tour of the Alamo. M.L.

walked outside and began to move toward the men. As he did so, they vanished! He looked everywhere but found no one. The next day, it dawned on him that not only had the men appeared to emerge from the rear wall of the chapel, which had no door or other opening, but that both men were dressed in what appeared to be home-spun clothing similar to the attire worn in the early 1800s. M.L. also recalled that he could "see through" both men, and though they were conversing, he never heard a sound.

Another time M.L. was walking through the cavalry courtyard located north of the long barracks. He distinctly heard someone walking behind him. Turning quickly in the direction of the sound, he was startled to see that no one was there. As M.L. continued making his rounds, the sound of footsteps trailing behind him returned. Abruptly spinning around for a second time, hoping to catch the prankster, M.L. was once again at a loss to find out who was shadowing him. By now, he was feeling both angry and helpless as he approached the north end of the museum gift shop. This time, without warning, he was literally "kicked" in the backside. He spun around while drawing his revolver, ready to finally put an end to this prank.

M.L. was stunned. He was staring blankly at the deserted grounds—no one was in sight. Immediately scanning the area, he realized that he was alone and helpless. As he stood and contemplated the situation, he heard the distinct sound of laughter echo through the empty courtyard. He also noticed a shadow darting near the rear entrance to the long barracks. M.L. immediately ran over to the spot where he had seen the shadow disappear; again, no one was in sight.

Whoever or whatever had followed and kicked M.L. had disappeared into the long barracks, never to be found. Being a nonbeliever when he first took the job at the

123

Alamo, M.L.'s initial skepticism about the unknown turned into a healthy respect for the twilight visitors who still roam the Alamo grounds. M.L. added that his next stint as a guard at the Alamo from 1988 to1989 produced no strange occurrences. Perhaps since he had become "a believer," there was no further need by the Alamo spirits to convince him that they were real!

A Wall of Tears

Spiritually, there are no answers. Many believe ghosts are earthbound spirits of people who have died. Often, at the sites of great emotion or sudden death, there are reports of ghosts. The reasons spirits stay earthbound are varied. Some people, when living, don't believe there is anything after this life. When they find themselves, as spirits, still aware and able to move, they are confused and don't know where to go. And if one does believe in heaven and hell, it's only logical that a small percentage of spirits might get lost on the way.

Laurie Jacobson and Marc Wanamaker,
Hollywood Haunted: A Ghostly Tour of Filmland (1994)

Former employee B.G. was willing to discuss a bizarre and profoundly melancholy experience she had while working in the gift shop. She remembered that the event took place in 1994 while she and a few fellow employees had to take inventory of the Alamo gift shop merchandise. Since a new basement had just been constructed under the gift shop, working within the cool confines of the subterranean storage area was quite pleasant—that is, until the chilling sounds of a woman weeping was heard from behind the walls.

A group of five employees began the inventory phase at the end of February, and although everyone was aware that this was the anniversary of the period that the Alamo had been under siege over a hundred and fifty years before, there was no indication that there would be any problem with undertaking this routine task—and it was routine until the sounds of a woman sobbing were heard by the

125

group. While they were counting books and other items, the sobbing became more intense, lasting hour after hour.

The haunted gift shop
Photograph by Robert Wlodarski

At first everyone looked at one another in disbelief and then searched the basement area to find the source of the sound—to no avail. The employees concluded that it was not coming from the area in which they were working. The mournful sound became so unnerving that one of the employees had to leave the basement and refused to return. The others had a job to do, and the fact that a woman was crying from within the walls of the basement could not keep them from their task. As the employees continued to inventory the merchandise, the wailing increased then decreased in intensity. It finally dawned on the group that the crying was in fact taking place around the time the battle had taken place almost one hundred and sixty years earlier.

A few of the women familiar with the history of the battle and aftermath surmised that the cries might be from one of the women who survived the Alamo attack but lost a husband or relative in the bloody struggle. Perhaps it was Juana Navarro de Alsbury who, with her sister, Gertrudis, and her infant son (her husband Dr. Horace Alsbury was away on a scouting mission) witnessed the carnage around her. One account has it that an Alamo defender named Mitchell tried to protect her during the height of the battle but was bayoneted by two Mexican soldiers. Also, a young Mexican defender attempted to use Juana as a shield and was also killed by the Mexicans. This act would certainly leave a lasting impression and a sense of sorrow, which may transcend death. Or the tears could belong to Susanna Arabella Dickinson, who may be crying over the death of her twenty-six-year-old husband, who was killed while manning the artillery battery at the rear of the chapel.

Another possibility is that the sounds might belong to Ana Salazar Esparza, who lost her husband, Gregorio, during the battle, choosing to stay by his side at the Alamo. José Gregorio Esparza manned the cannon for the defenders during the battle close to where his wife, Ana, was sheltered. Gregorio's body was found by his brother, Francisco, who was a member of General Cos's troops but took an oath that he was not willing to join the Mexican forces. Gregorio was felled by a bullet to the chest as well as stabbed in the side by a sword. From a paranormal standpoint, the possibilities pertaining to the sounds of a woman crying within an area where an intense battle was fought are endless considering how men and women from both sides lost family members as a result of the battle.

B.G. continued her story by pronouncing that the strange and mournful cries lasted for two straight days (February 27 and 28), continuing periodically while the inventory took place. Other employees could not stay long in the basement because the crying was so mournful that it would leave them in tears. Unfortunately for the staff, the crying was not the only "strange incident" that occurred in the basement. On rare occasions, the women would also see shadows emerge on the walls and disappear, always leaving them chilled to the bone and without any explanation. The shadows would seem to follow the employees, leaving a clearly visible outline of a body on the walls. When employees turned to see who was there, they found only stillness and emptiness.

Occasionally, a shadow would follow employees upstairs and into the gift shop after hours. Everyone was in agreement that the episodes were "bizarre" and "eerie," but no one felt threatened and most grew accustomed to their unseen guests. The unsettling crying episodes, which ended after a few days, left an indelible imprint on the psyche of those who experienced it. B.G. believed that the elusive shadows and particularly the mournful crying might have been related to the Alamo battle, especially since the incidents occurred at around the time the battle would have taken place in 1836. Beyond this general speculation, there are no logical explanations for the "wall of tears."

Guard (Dead) Moments

The American Heritage Dictionary of the English Language defines the word specter as "a ghost, phantom, apparition. A mental image, phantasm. A foreboding." That will do although some of our contacts prefer the word "presence" which they feel is more indicative of the sensation of energy or being present, if sometimes unseen.

Margaret Wayt DeBolt, *Savannah Spectres and Other Strange Tales* (1984)

A former ranger shared a few of his experiences while working within the Alamo confines. His first experience occurred during the summer of 1975 while working in the security office. It was around 2 or 3 A.M., recalled the skeptical man. Not one to be frightened easily and certainly not afraid of the rumors of ghosts wandering the hollowed Alamo grounds, the ranger nevertheless encountered the unexplainable.

While sitting in the security office (then called the "Old Green House," located approximately twenty feet from the present-day security office), the ranger chanced to look out the window toward the chapel. He watched incredulously as a man walked across the grounds near the acequia and disappeared behind a cottonwood tree. Because there was a full moon out, the ranger was able to discern that the man was tall, slender, and wore a three-cornered hat (circa early 1800s) as he nonchalantly crossed the Alamo grounds. The ranger remembered that it was a quiet night—not a breath of wind. He immediately jumped up from behind his desk and, after grabbing his flashlight, ran out in search of the "trespasser." He hurried to where he had seen the odd-looking fellow near the acequia. He found no one but stated that the hair on the back of his neck and arms stood up. As he secured the area, the ranger proceeded to check every nook and cranny. Whatever he saw had literally vanished. He had no explanations and did not report the incident.

Another time, the ranger was confronted by M.H., a fellow ranger, who seemed to have something on his mind but was reluctant to talk about it. The ranger encouraged M.H. to open up, and M.H. responded that while he was on the "dog watch" (a nickname for the late-night shift) around midnight, he was standing on the bridge by the acequia. There, he saw a man standing by some flowering

The Acequia in the foreground, the gift shop in the background
Photograph by Rober Wlodarski

bushes. M.H. shouted "Halt!" three times to the intruder. On the third shout, a distracted M.H. turned away for a split second. Returning his gaze to where the intruder had been standing, he was shocked to see that the man had disappeared. He looked quickly in all directions, realizing that it was impossible for anyone to vanish that quickly. M.H. and his co-worker reassured each other that there were unexplainable things going on at the Alamo, and there was nothing they could do about it.

It was also the former ranger's duty to take down the Texas and United States flags each afternoon at 4:30 P.M. After folding them, he always took the flags into the chapel and laid them neatly on the information desk. On one occasion, after folding the flags, placing them on the desk, and locking up at 5:30, the ranger distinctly remembered glancing over at the desk to see that the flags were still folded and in their proper place. The next morning, at 6:00 A.M., the ranger unlocked the door and entered the chapel. To his amazement, although the flags were still neatly folded, they were now down on the floor instead of lying on the desk! There was no way anyone could get in or out of the chapel once it was locked because the alarm system would have been triggered. There was no explanation for what had occurred. It was as if someone had picked up the flags from the desk and neatly laid them down on the floor and walked away. The ranger then stated that several times when he or other guards would open the chapel door and walk in, there was a strong feeling that someone was walking alongside or behind them. Sometimes their hair stood on end; other times a light gust of air would gently brush by them. They could all feel a presence when alone in the chapel.

The chapel was also the place where three other odd incidents occurred to the former ranger. Once, upon entering the chapel early in the morning, he found a puddle of

Rear of the chapel—north-facing exit across from the gift shop
Photograph by Robert Wlodarski

water on the floor near the southwest corner of the building. It had not rained, and there were no known leaks of any kind. What had caused the puddle of water was never determined, but when the maintenance man was called, he refused to go in and mop up the water without the ranger staying inside with him. The maintenance men were well aware of the mysterious events that had been reported over the years, and this particular man was not going to remain inside, even for a few minutes, without a fellow human being standing nearby. The mysterious water spot was mopped up but never explained away.

The second incident involved the presence of dirt inside the chapel. Once again, the ranger opened the chapel door early one morning and to his shock, found several small piles of dirt on the floor in the two end rooms of the chapel. There were no footprints leading away from the dirt piles. A janitor was again called in to clean up the mess. As with the water incident, the man refused to remain in the room alone. Again, the former ranger had to stand guard while the janitor completed his task. This incident also was never explained. As an aside, the rangers adopted a cat named Ruby. Over the years, the cat developed a sixth sense and, upon entering the chapel, her hair would often stand on end.

Other miscellaneous experiences were related by this ranger: Murmurs, whispers, and strange sounds such as tin cups banging on the wall were sometimes heard coming from the old well in front of the long barracks. Words, short phrases, and mumbling sounding like a "bunch of drunks" have been heard in the long barracks at night by a number of guards. This is impossible because the area is constantly patrolled each night and has a built-in alarm system. On a number of occasions, guards have observed visitors walking into the long barracks and quickly exiting with disturbed expressions on their faces. Also, in the long barracks, guards have reported artifacts, which are locked in cases, being moved from one case to another, which is rather odd as it occurs at night when the barracks are locked and secured.

A final anecdote related by the former ranger concerned a light in the window directly above the chapel door. It was late one evening when a light in the window caught the ranger's attention. He moved closer to investigate. No one was supposed to be inside, and the lights in the chapel had been turned off. He looked around, checking out possible explanations such as reflections from cars or exterior lighting. As he moved closer, the light disappeared. He decided to have a look inside just to be sure that no one had broken in. The building was empty, and the former ranger returned to his post. A short time later, the ranger saw the light again. Knowing that no one was inside and determining that external light sources were not to blame, he simply chose to ignore the phantom light.

As an aside, one of the authors and a family member were standing in front of the Alamo around midnight when they witnessed this light in the same location that the former ranger described. It was there for a few beats, then went out. The former ranger ended his stories by stating, "You can stand out here (in front of the chapel) past midnight, and these lights will go out, and you can sense that there's something under this ground."

Images of the Past

As researchers, we have had several people tell us that they have captured Alamo ghosts on film (unfortunately, to date, no one has sent us a single photograph). A majority of the stories associated with Alamo ghost photos involve unsuspecting tourists who have inadvertently captured strange hazes, mysterious balls and streaks of light, and phantom-like images of soldiers, defenders, a ghostly child, and unidentifiable shapes. One female visitor said she snapped a picture of the west-facing exterior of the gift shop while standing in the area between the gift shop and long barracks in the well courtyard. As she stood there, camera in hand, she saw nothing as she took the photograph; however, when it was developed, the face of a young boy appeared in one of the windows. Regrettably, she entrusted the picture to someone in order to have it authenticated—it was never returned. No doubt, this is the same little boy who has been repeatedly spotted peering down at tourists and rangers for many years.

It seems as if every individual we talked to who had a ghostly photo story was taking a photograph of a seemingly innocuous setting, such as the exterior of the chapel, long barracks, gift shop, acequia, north courtyard, well courtyard, or the inner courtyards and gardens. Although these individuals swear that when they took the photographs there was nothing visibly odd or strange in the background, upon developing the film, something unexplainable is captured.

Over the years, other individuals have reported seeing ghostly figures of buckskin-clad men or formless phantoms standing or walking throughout the Alamo grounds.

One shocked tourist reported what he described as two Mexican soldiers standing at attention near the long barracks—they were there one minute, gone the next. On another occasion, a young boy taking a family photograph captured a murky image of what appeared to be an Alamo defender floating about six inches above the ground near the rear of the chapel. Another common sighting, also caught on film, is that of a person's face, an individual described as a male, whose partial figure materializes in one of the windows above the entrance to the chapel. Similar to the ghostly child who appears in the gift shop windows, there is no way an individual could stand in that area of the chapel given the physical constraints of the setting.

Ghost photographs are not an everyday occurrence, yet some people appear to be more in tune to capturing spirits on film than others; or the spirits simply choose to manifest themselves to certain individuals, on certain days, under particular conditions. So, the next time you visit the Alamo, go ahead, take your best shot!

What Lurks in the Basement?

Two former employees encountered what they described as a male and female spirit in the gift shop basement while they were taking inventory. One of the spirits seems to be that of a Native American woman, because the employees saw what looked liked a headdress with feathers gracing the image. The male phantom may have been a soldier, since he was described as short and barrel-chested, and he seemed to be leaning on a rifle. Both women said the events were under thirty seconds in duration, and although the images seemed to be hazy or misty, the women could make out some of the features.

Phantoms are not the only strange and eerie things that cause the staff concern when they descend into the basement. Frequently, an intense weeping, sobbing, and moaning fills the room, as if it is coming from inside the basement walls. The depressing sound will last for about a minute or less in most cases, then cease. One employee said the crying sounds are like those of a woman in mourning, perhaps distraught over a loved one who died during the battle. According to several of the staff, the unexplainable sounds increase in frequency during late February and March—the time of the battle in 1836.

An event which occurs frequently to many employees who venture into the gift shop basement is that of a pervasive, almost oppressive feeling of being watched or followed. This is sometimes accompanied by formless shadows gliding on the wall alongside the unsuspecting staff person. This hair-raising feeling of being watched startles and perturbs some of the employees, while scaring the daylights out of others. More often than not, however, the persons turn in the perceived direction of the "feeling," only to find themselves alone—yet they are sure they're not.

This unnatural feeling of being watched by an unseen force, combined with sudden cold spots or a case of the chills, makes the basement a rather foreboding place to work in. The women emphasized that this is by no means an everyday event, and not everyone feels the presence, but it has happened to a number of people over the years.

Why the basement of the gift shop? Do the occasional manifestations have something to do with the mysterious underground tunnels, which some say existed at the time of the battle? Was the gift shop built on top of a part of the battlefield that had extremely heavy casualties? Only the spirits know for sure.

A Brief Tour of Duty

A number of current and former rangers have Alamo ghost stories to tell; however, they are extremely hesitant to talk about their experiences for fear of being ridiculed by others—particularly fellow rangers who have never had a similar experience. Some of those who have talked to us confirm that many more rangers have had "supernatural" experiences but fear people will laugh at them or refuse to associate with them. The fact of the matter is many of these law enforcement officers have had something unusual or inexplicable happen to them while on duty. They are only now coming forward because others have "broken the ice," albeit anonymously.

A majority of the encounters between the 1836 Alamo defenders, and those who work to guard, protect, or maintain this sacred Texas monument occur during the "dog watch"—that bewitching time between midnight and three in the morning when the spirits are very active and seem to most often manifest. The dog watch is also known by the those who patrol the grounds, as the "ghost-watch." Perhaps the atmospheric conditions, the darkness, time of year, or other factors contribute to the increase in paranormal activity between midnight and three. Maybe, it's the individual. Whatever the reason it is the time one is most likely to encounter the other dimension.

One ranger we'll call Sam, while on dog watch, had an encounter with the unknown during a cool, spring evening. The area between the gift shop and the cavalry courtyard seems to be a "highly charged" and paranormally active area where many sightings have occurred over the years. It was in this area that the young ranger first became aware of the supernatural. It began innocently enough with a cold spot noticeably colder than the location the ranger had previously occupied. Sam, feeling the temperature change, stopped on the spot and looked around. Just prior to this, Sam had the distinct feeling of being followed. The combination of the intense cold, the feeling of being followed or watched, and the stories that had circulated about strange and unusual things occurring to a number of fellow rangers over the years were taking their toll on Sam's psyche. Surely the ghostly tales were just that. Weren't they? Sam was now feeling a little uneasy.

Having worked there only a short time, never before had Sam encountered anything remotely similar to what other rangers talked about among themselves after their shifts had concluded. The cold spots, apparitions, disembodied voices, noises, and feelings of being watched and even touched by unseen hands—but this was different. This was happening now! Although Sam continued making the rounds, the feeling of being followed remained during the entire watch. In fact, it was the beginning of a series of strange events that continued until it proved to be too much. Unable to transfer to a day shift, the ranger decided to call it quits.

As Sam was leaving for a new job assignment, a ranger offered a bit of consolation: Although most of the rangers never really get used to working the late shift, some just ignore the weird events, while others leave the haunted Alamo never to return. Sam wouldn't be the first or last ranger to have a brief tour of duty.

Not Present But Accounted For

Another apparition who frequents the Alamo grounds is a young man wearing a western duster. He seems content to stand around with a far-off gaze, then disappear. This ghost is oftentimes only visible as a hazy or transparent image, although he sometimes appears soaking wet, as if he came in out of the rain; however, there is never a cloud in the sky when he is sighted.

The summers of 1997 and 1998 produced several sightings of this Alamo phantom. According to one visiting couple, on a sweltering, humid afternoon, around 2:00 P.M. they saw an odd-looking man in a full-length, western coat, standing near the back entrance to the chapel. The fact that everyone else was attired in shorts and tee shirts and the temperature was close to 100 degrees caused the couple to almost laugh at the absurdity of the sight standing before them. They thought at first the man might be a "flasher," then they noticed that he was soaking wet from head to toe. Perhaps he was a misguided groundskeeper or an Alamo re-enactor trying to give tourists a taste of history when wearing shorts was not an option.

The couple watched the strange figure for over a minute. He just stood there in the sweltering sun, not even flinching and not looking at anything in particular. Just as they were about to take a few steps toward the man, he vanished in front of their bewildered eyes. The couple quickly rushed over to the area where the man had been standing. A quick look around the immediate area produced nothing. The odd man in the western duster was simply nowhere to be found. The couple was baffled and thought perhaps they had been standing in the sun too long. Maybe it was the sun, and maybe it was something out of the ordinary. Whatever the cause, it was a trip they would never forget.

Two rangers also talked about their unforgettable encounter with a strange-looking gentleman wearing a long coat. One ranger, making his rounds late at night, observed the man standing as still as death on the grounds near the library, wearing period attire from the 1800s, on the grounds near the Alamo hall and library. He thought to himself how odd the entire scene was: It was a very cool night; the man appeared to be drenched to the bone; he was standing alone and staring blankly into the night, looking quite real; then he vanished as the curious ranger approached. As usual, a thorough inspection of the grounds for evidence of any intruder produced nothing.

A second ranger produced a similar report of the phantom. The second ranger also witnessed an odd-looking man of average height, wearing a long coat from the Wild West days, standing alone near the northern wall of the library. The gentleman was sopping wet and staring into the darkness, when he vanished into thin air. Once again, a search of the grounds yielded no one fitting that description.

Who is this stranger in the night from another era? Is he one of the Alamo defenders standing perpetual guard near the spot where he died? Is he someone who lived in the area prior to the battle, an early settler perhaps? One thing is certain: His body may not be present in this world, but his spirit is accounted for, as evidenced by the number of eyewitnesses who continue to spot him on the hallowed Alamo grounds.

Window to the Soul

Another commonly reported ghostly tale is that of seeing a haunting face, strange lights, or a partial apparition in one of the three upper-floor chapel windows. A quick walk inside the chapel will prove that there is no physical way a person could actually stand in either of the three windows (there is no ledge or ladder inside, and the drop to the floor of a considerable distance). Therefore, the stories seem to point to another Alamo spirit.

Today, there are five upper-story chapel windows. Three openings were part of the original structural design; two were constructed as recessed ornamental openings, which probably held statues; and a third window, larger, almost square-framed, stood directly above the entryway to the chapel. Two additional, smaller, rectangular windows were added later by the U.S. Army around 1847-1848. The addition of two more windows coincided with the later construction of the famous parapet that has become the trademark of the chapel and is incorporated in the Alamo legend. The added windows were placed to the left and right of the existing ornamental window openings.

At the time of the battle, a man was probably posted at the window above the chapel door, with several cannons placed on the roof providing an excellent vantage point of the field of battle below. The appearance of unexplainable shapes, mysterious lights, murky-featured faces, and phantom images at the chapel windows does not seem unreasonable considering the intense fighting that occurred in that area during the battle, especially during the last stand. A number of Alamo defenders and Mexican soldiers lost their lives inside the building as well as just

143

outside the chapel doors between the wood palisade and the long barracks.

Perhaps some of the images, lights, and apparitions that have been sighted over the years represent a defender or defenders who are standing watch prior to the ensuing battle. Or they are men killed during the battle who are not yet aware that the battle is over and they are dead. It is possible that the energy may even precede the battle of the Alamo and represents Native Americans, monks, neophytes, Spaniards, or early settlers who were buried in front of the chapel.

During a recent sighting, a twelve-year-old girl, while taking a ghost tour with her father, began shouting excitedly and questioning him about the man who was staring at her from the window above the entryway to the chapel. The startled father looked up quickly, but he saw no one. On another occasion, a man and his wife related a similar story about someone, a hazy image, looking down on them from the chapel window. He was there one minute, then he vanished. Finally, an eight-year-old girl, while waiting for a ghost tour with her parents (at around 11:00 P.M.), reported seeing a man standing in one of the upper windows looking out over the group, then suddenly vanishing.

The general description of the mysterious specter is that of a man, clean-shaven and hatless, looking out of one of the upper windows at those standing below. Most sightings seem to occur within a 20- to 45-second time frame. In some cases the apparition quickly vanishes as people are watching, while in other cases, a person turns away to tell others, usually a matter of seconds, then turns back to find that the apparition has then disappeared.

There's No One Out There

In August of 1998 two teenage girls from Austin, Texas, were taking the Hauntings History Ghost Tour of San Antonio conducted by ghost hunter Martin Leal. During the tour the girls were off on their own but still within earshot of the tour group when they encountered the ghostly child who haunts the gift shop. According to Leal, the girls had entered gate one and were walking along the path in the well courtyard between the Alamo chapel and the long barracks. As they reached the area near a remnant of the reconstructed wall on top of the early mission foundations, they happened to look up at the west-facing portion of the gift shop windows.

They were startled to see the face of a little boy looking down at them from the upper story window. Although the distance between them and the window prevented a more accurate recollection of the boy's features, both girls described the young boy as being around ten or twelve years old, conforming to psychic Kathleen Bittner's earlier impression of the child. It also coincided with other accounts of the phantom boy. However, when the girls told their mothers about their experience, the adults scoffed at the possibility of seeing a spirit. When Leal showed the family a book that included other stories about the ghost child, the young girls were relieved that someone believed them, or more to the point, that others had shared a similar experience—one that continues to this day. Although their mothers were adamant that no one could have been peering out of the window, and ghosts did not exist, Leal and the girls shot each other knowing smiles—they knew better!

The Ghost and the Ghost Hunter

Martin Leal also had an eerie encounter while visiting the Alamo. He was talking to a ranger and two women from Denver, Colorado, around 11:00 P.M. Out of the corner of his eye, he saw a dark image from the waist up above the wall to the left of gate one. The image only lasted for a couple of seconds, then quickly vanished. According to Leal, it happened so fast that there was no way a person could have possibly ducked down below the wall or run away. He clearly saw someone standing near the wall.

Leal then walked over and told a ranger that he saw a person standing on the wall near the north courtyard, knowing that if he said he had seen a ghost, the ranger would have ignored him. As Leal ran to the gate and looked in, the ranger came over, unlocked gate one, and went inside and looked around the area near the well. When the ranger returned after a few minutes, he told Leal that he must have imagined the whole thing, because he searched everywhere and there was no sign of anyone anywhere on the grounds. It happened so fast that Leal wondered if he really had seen the ghost.

Two weeks later a woman who had gone on one of Leal's ghost tours the night before confided in Leal that she had witnessed something strange while on his tour. The woman told him that as she was positioned at gate one around 10:00 P.M. and looking around at the long barracks toward the well, she saw a dark shadowy figure standing on the other side of it. The woman said that she reported it to the ranger on duty with the same results as Leal—no intruder was found. Her description was similar to Leal's—she had seen a man about five feet, six inches tall, wearing what appeared to be period clothing, and he had vanished in front of their eyes.

It's Never Too Early for Spirits

According to a number of researchers ghosts are more likely to be spotted at night than in the morning. At least that is what a woman we'll call V.M. thought as she nonchalantly entered the gift shop basement at 10:00 A.M. She was taking her first break of the day. As usual, she headed downstairs to her locker to get money out of her purse before walking across the street to grab a bite to eat. As she opened her locker, V.M. suddenly experienced a cold gust of air flow by her, and worse yet, she suddenly had an overwhelming feeling that someone was in the room with her. But that couldn't be; V.M. knew that she was the only one on break and that everyone else was supposed to be upstairs working. As frightened as she was at that instant, curiosity got the better of her. It was imperative for her to see who was watching her, even though her "sixth sense" told her that what she was about to witness would not be human.

As V.M. slowly turned around, she was greeted by a hazy, almost smoky gray image standing in front of her. She remarked that the cloudy image looked as if someone had taken a black, felt-tipped marker and drawn an outline around the image. Feeling something between panic and curiosity, V.M. was able to determine that the figure was that of a man wearing a high hat with feather-like objects protruding from the top. She said it resembled the outfit that most historians had portrayed Santa Anna wearing during the battle of the Alamo. As the image seemed to just hover in front of her, if took all of V.M.'s energy to run around the floating apparition and make it up the stairs. She was too frightened to turn back and see if it was following her. As she reached the comfort of the well-lit gift shop, she was frantic and winded. She worried little about her open locker or her purse.

At the top of the stairs, V.M. was greeted by a fellow employee, who saw her condition and commented that she looked "white as a ghost." That's when V.M. told the employee what had happened to her in the basement. After relating the story to her co-worker and resting at the top of the stairs, V.M. recovered enough to return to the ghostly scene; however, this time, V.M. would take two other employees with her. As it turned out, while V.M. was reacting to the apparition, another employee was going down to the break room via the elevator. As the woman stepped out of the elevator, she watched V.M. scurry up the stairs. Thinking something was wrong, she followed V.M. up the stairs. The three women were conferring about the incident and about returning to the basement.

As the three women returned to the spot where the event occurred, there was no sign of the ethereal image resembling Santa Anna. However, the woman from the elevator related the fact that although she had never seen an apparition in the basement area, on a number of occasions she had heard mysterious crying sounds coming from one of the storerooms. Every time she was brave enough to inspect the area, she found no one. It was as if the sounds were coming from inside the very walls of the storeroom.

V.M. didn't care to hear about the mysterious sounds. She had enough problems dealing with her apparitional encounter. For V.M., there would be no more trips to the basement without the company of another human. She had discovered that spirits don't always wait for late hours to appear.

The Crying Game

A coworker had a strange experience with V.M. on another occasion in the basement area. As both women were in one of the stock rooms below the gift shop, the coworker began hearing a faint, crying sound. The cry was barely audible, low-pitched and soft, and sounded like a small child wanting attention or, perhaps, to be fed. When it began, both women looked at one another as if to say, "Do you hear that?" After a few minutes, the crying became louder. This was the first time V.M. had heard the sound, but her coworker had gone through this a number of times in the past. As the sounds continued, V.M. wanted to leave the area immediately, but the woman asked her to stay and listen for a few more minutes—V.M. reluctantly agreed.

As V.M. and the coworker stood in the storeroom, the child's cry became stronger. The gentle cry soon changed to a loud, painful wail. The sound came from nowhere in particular, yet it surrounded the women. As the crying became more intense, V.M. remembers feeling frightened. After a few minutes, she decided that she'd had enough. The coworker, however, seemed fascinated by the crying. Apparently the strange noise begins at a barely audible frequency, increases for a few minutes, then stops abruptly. One janitor has heard the sounds but attributes them to stray cats. The women know better; to them, the sound is definitely the mournful cry of an other-worldly child, somehow trapped in time in the basement of the gift shop.

A Clean Sweep

Not long ago, a new female employee we'll call Wendy was asked to clean up some of the exhibits in the long barracks after closing time. Tourists wandering through the hallowed barracks tend to want to get as close to the artifacts there as they possibly can, and they leave smeared and smudged fingerprints on the glass cases. The job seemed simple enough—make sure that the cases were cleaned for the next round of tourists. As Wendy proceeded walking through the long barracks from south to north, she heard the distinct sound of a strong cough. She was sure that it belonged to a man. As Wendy turned to check out the source, she heard the coughing sound once again; this time it was coming from the southern portion of the barracks. She thought to herself that it was a bad cough, a guttural, painful cough, as if someone were on his deathbed.

As Wendy slowly made her way past the display cases, the coughing continued, and she began picking up the strong smell of whiskey in the air. After making a clean sweep of the entire long barracks, she found no one. The coughing, however, continued, and now the smell of alcohol became overwhelming. The windows were tightly shut, so she knew that the smell could not be coming from the outside; so where then, she asked herself? A few more minutes, several coughs, and the choking smell of whiskey drove Wendy out of the long barracks. Enough was enough. She was getting spooked! The cleaning was put on hold, and she told her supervisor what had happened. Wendy was startled to hear that others had experienced the coughing sounds, as well as the smell of alcohol throughout the barracks. Wendy was then told about Jim

151

Bowie's last, painful days at the Alamo, where he lay in a cot, drinking whiskey and coughing.

Is Jim Bowie's ghost responsible for some of the strange noises that rangers and employees frequently hear inside the long barracks? Considering that Bowie's last moments on earth were horrendous, perhaps his psychic imprint lingers for others to hear and perhaps take pity on his restless soul. Unfortunately for those who administer to the cleaning and protection of the long barracks, Bowie's spirit is not the only one that has been sighted or heard inside. A clean sweep of the area seems to turn up more than just a few cobwebs. Like Wendy's experience, the long barracks is filled with paranormal events attributed to the last stand.

A Stacked Deck

For V.M. and several coworkers, it had been a long and grueling day working in the gift shop. It was Saturday evening, and they had to come right back again on Sunday. The group locked up the gift shop at 5:30 P.M. and activated the security system—no one stayed behind. They all returned early the next morning to open up. As they passed through the entrance corridor and entered the main area, they stood speechless. Before them was a stack of postcards on the countertop, neatly piled one on top of the other—several feet high. The nearby postcard racks had been completely emptied. The startled women looked at one another and then quickly looked around the shop to see if someone had come in and played a prank.

Their suspicion immediately fell on the rangers. The ladies thought the rangers might have come in early and stacked the cards in order to scare or tease them. However, after careful consideration they realized that the rangers wouldn't or couldn't have done this. Since there are security cameras set up inside the gift shop that would have caught the rangers playing the practical joke, they admitted to themselves that they would not have had time to do it, and why would they take all that time to neatly stack the cards and possibly risk losing their jobs over a practical joke.

The rangers who were on duty that night were thoroughly questioned but were adamant about their innocence. They said when they made their early morning inspection of the gift shop everything was in order. There were no cards out of place, and nothing was out of the ordinary. So, who or what took all the postcards from the racks and stacked them in a nice, neat pile for the ladies to see when they arrived on Sunday morning? Nobody ever found the culprit, and nothing showed up on the security camera. The cards were in the rack one minute, then the deck was stacked.

All's Well That Ends Well

During a casual conversation between a gift shop employee and ghost hunter Martin Leal, the employee told Leal that one day, as the gift shop director left her office for the day, she was stopped on her way out of the Alamo grounds by an elderly lady sitting on a bench near gate one. The lady proceeded to tell the director how much she enjoyed her visit to the Alamo and how she especially enjoyed the re-enactor who was dressed in an 1800s costume, similar to what the Alamo defenders would have been wearing during their last days, and stood under the large tree by the well. Apparently, the lady saw the man greeting visitors as they entered and left the area. She said adding that little touch of authenticity to the tour made her trip to the sacred shrine that much more enjoyable; it was a trip she would highly recommend to her friends. She also said to thank the young man for doing such a commendable job.

The director thanked the woman for her kind comments, then left, shaking her head as she exited gate one. Who is the spirit continually spotted near the well? Perhaps it is an Alamo defender preparing for a battle that continues to be played out in another dimension, and he simply takes a few moments to greet those who pass by in this dimension. For the elderly lady and the gift shop director, all's well that ends well.

Wasn't That You?

On one occasion, a tour guide had completed the last tour of the long barracks and was in the process of locking up when his friend approached him with a strange question: "What did you forget." The second guide had no idea what his friend was talking about. The first guide explained how he had taken the last group of tourists through and had gone through the usual lockup procedures. After he finished, he was standing near the far end of the north courtyard facing Houston Street when he distinctly saw the other guide, or what he thought was the other guide, make a quick dash toward the north door of the long barracks and enter. He thought that the other guide must have left something important inside. After a few minutes he noticed that no one came out, so he investigated.

He reopened the north door and walked in. He called for his friend, but there was no answer. Thinking that his friend was playing a joke on him, he walked through the entire building. He heard his name called and once again reacted by calling out to his friend to come and stop teasing him. The guide searched everywhere but couldn't find anyone hiding. The other doors were locked, so it would have been impossible for anyone to get past him. After several more minutes, he was getting a little "spooked," so he left and locked up.

After both guides discussed the incident and checked inside the long barracks one more time, they realized that what the one guide witnessed was not the other guide, but someone who passed through the area, entered the locked back door, and vanished inside.

156

The Joke's on You

There's an unspoken rule that when dealing with the unknown, one does not mock the spirits. However, a couple of rangers did just that, and the spirits retaliated. As the story goes, two rangers were summoned to the chapel one night at around 10:00 P.M. when the lights mysteriously went out inside. Since the area is considered to be the most sacred spot on the grounds, the rangers respond immediately to a potential vandal or a break-in. As the rangers entered, they used their flashlights while power was being restored. As they walked through the chapel (an eerie experience even during daylight hours) they were teasing one another, saying "Boo" and playfully joking around to ease the tension.

The two rangers went from the entrance, through the nave, and to the rear of the chapel without incident. They found no one else inside, nothing amiss, and no sounds of an intruder trying to hide out. On their way back, as the rangers passed the former sacristy and monk's burial ground (where dozens of flags are exhibited), they stopped dead in their tracks. Their teasing remarks abruptly stopped as they first heard what seemed like chanting and barely audible voices, followed by a bright, bluish light emanating from the monk's burial ground enclave. The rangers wasted little time in locking up and hurrying out of the chapel. They did not bother to inspect the source of the light or where the strange voices were coming from—if it were an intruder, the person could stay put if he or she liked. Reaching the exterior entrance to the chapel, the rangers vowed never to make fun of the ghosts again. This time, the joke was on them!

157

The Phantom

There are a number of gates that allow access to the Alamo grounds from Crockett, Bonham, Houston, and North Alamo Street, beginning with gate one located between the chapel and long barracks. The gate opens into what would have been the convent yard/horse quarters, cattle pen, convent, and hospital during the siege. This was also the area where the defenders made the last stand and the heaviest fighting during the battle took place. It is where some believe Davy Crockett fell during the battle.

Gate one is known for its paranormal occurrences, where shadows, apparitions, and floating images are occasionally seen by unsuspecting rangers and tourists alike, both in sunlight as well as in the dead of night. One ranger told Martin Leal of an encounter he'd had with a shadowy figure near the cavalry courtyard one November evening. According to the ranger, he was making his usual rounds with a fellow ranger, who was patrolling another area, when he reached gate one. From that vantage point, he could look out toward the chapel, the front lawn area, and the park fronting North Alamo Street. As the ranger stood there for a moment, he felt as if he were being watched. Thinking it was his partner, who had already completed his rounds, the ranger turned quickly to say something to the fellow ranger. There was no one there. As he peered into the darkness, he noticed a figure or the shadow of a figure move toward the long barracks. He reasoned that if it was not his partner, perhaps someone had climbed the fence and broken in and was hiding near a wall or in the brush.

The ranger gave pursuit but never found a thing. Since the long barracks is secured each night, no one could have gotten inside, and since the ranger gave pursuit immediately, no one would have been able to escape that quickly. His partner finally arrived, and the ranger told him what had just happened. The other ranger listened patiently and after the story was finished, just shrugged his shoulders and said, "Oh, that's just the phantom who hangs out over there."

A Lower-Level Encounter

One Alamo ranger thought he had seen it all during his years of loyal service. He had protected the Alamo against vandals, fanatics, avid partygoers, rambunctious tourists, and the overly curious. However, there was one thing he was never trained to guard against—ghosts! This ranger recounted his experience with the unknown, adamantly prefacing the story with, "I do not believe in spirits and such." The ranger had no logical explanation for what had happened to him.

According to the former ranger, it was an autumn night sometime after eleven. He was patrolling the grounds that night with another ranger. Having made his rounds past gate one, the long barracks, well courtyard, and north courtyard, he was proceeding toward the gift shop when he clearly saw a man run from the side entrance to the chapel toward the gift shop and disappear. He instinctively called for backup, thinking that a vandal had entered the grounds. As he waited for help, he walked around the gift shop building and ended up at the front door. It was then that he heard someone inside. As he stood there waiting for the other ranger to provide assistance, he kept wondering how someone could have run that quickly across the courtyard area and broken into the locked gift shop. The ranger was even more confused when his partner came and he explained that the door was secure and had not been broken into; furthermore, the alarm had not sounded. As the two rangers stood outside, contemplating what they should do next, they both heard a noise come from behind the locked door!

Without wasting time, they neutralized the alarm and quickly unlocked the door. After hesitating a split second, not sure what would greet them once the door was opened, they nervously entered with their flashlights readied. Beams of light filled the entryway as they stood inside. It was deathly quiet, and the air was unusually musty. The two men split up and began inspecting the adjoining offices and the main shop area. One ranger checked out the back area, and rear entry from East Houston Street facing the Emily Morgan Hotel. Nothing had been broken into, and the door was securely locked. In the meantime, the other ranger, our storyteller, heard a noise coming from behind the door leading to the basement. He was sure he had his man. With his flashlight in one hand and the other hand on the door, he pulled hard, expecting the door to be open. It didn't budge. It was still locked! The ranger wondered how someone could have so quickly entered two locked doors and relocked them without keys. Was someone playing a joke on him?

The ranger proceeded to unlock the door and open it. Before taking a step, he shined his flashlight down the steps. In that instant, he felt a blast of extremely cold air pass right through him. At the same time, a beam of light from his flashlight struck a target. He had his intruder; or so he thought. Directly in front of him was the figure of a man dressed in buckskin clothing, looking directly up at him. As their eyes met for an instant, the beam from his flashlight penetrated the man and then the figure vanished. The startled ranger's mouth dropped as his light now pierced only darkness. There was no way he was going down in the basement to try and find out where his intruder went, so he did an immediate 180 degree turn, exited the door, locked it, and called to his partner. The cold air dissipated as his partner came running over.

161

As they discussed his story, the rangers shook their heads in disbelief. They had heard ghostly tales, but never had anything unusual happened to them before. The rangers quickly locked up the gift shop and went back to patrolling the grounds. The ranger who witnessed the event referred to it as a hallucination, blaming it on a lack of sleep the night before. The two rangers never spoke about the incident to their boss for fear of being ridiculed or fired. The ranger's hallucination, as he called it, has been shared by too many others to be discounted. The lower-level encounters continue to produce occasional surprises for unsuspecting rangers and other staff members.

Additional Accounts

Ghosts are concerned with what happened to them, rather than where it happened. In most accounts of hauntings, the spirit comes back to erase, re-enact, avenge, or simply brood about an event or unfulfilled longing.

Antoinette May, *Haunted Houses of California* (1990)

Another former Alamo ranger recalled standing at the entrance gate one evening looking out toward the plaza. As he was locking up, an uneasy sensation overcame him, causing him to turn around. Although his view of the grounds was partially blocked by portions of standing architectural features, what he saw happening in front of him for a few brief moments came from an unobstructed vantage point. As the ranger turned to look toward the Alamo grounds, he clearly and distinctly saw a man darting across the area between the long barracks and the chapel.

As the ranger continued to follow the movement of the individual, he noticed that the man appeared to be floating rather than running. As he looked below the figure's knees, the ranger observed that it had no legs. Instead of running, the figure seemed to "drift" or "glide" diagonally from the long barracks toward the chapel, passing through a tree, then vanished from view behind the chapel. After "regrouping," the ranger quickly gave chase to the phantom form. Upon reaching the location where the figure was last observed, the ranger conducted a careful search of the entire grounds including the chapel without so much

163

The haunted courtyard between the chapel and long barracks
Photograph by Robert Wlodarski

as a glimpse of the elusive man figure—it had simply vaporized before his eyes.

One day, three maintenance men were performing repair work in a corridor near gate five, which lies between the chapel and long barracks. While relaxing during their lunch break, the workers watched in stunned silence as a figure of a man in buckskin walked toward them, made an abrupt ninety-degree turn, and passed through the wall. Exchanged looks of bewilderment and disbelief quickly changed to curiosity, and the three men hastened to the spot where the mystery man had disappeared.

Responding like a team of highly trained detectives, they thoroughly inspected both sides of the wall as well as any possible openings in an attempt to determine if what they thought they saw could really have taken place. The inspection proved that what they saw could not be explained away. There were no doors, gates or other passages that would have provided a means for the figure to escape. The phantom had somehow "walked" right through a stone wall! The workers knew what they had witnessed, and although it might have crossed their minds that they may have seen a ghost, no one was willing to verbalize it. The three men remained apprehensive and alert the rest of the day, occasionally glancing over their shoulders and hoping for another glimpse of their "unearthly" visitor. Unfortunately, they did not see any more unusual occurrences during the remainder of the job.

A former ranger claimed that it was easy to tell when "something strange" was going to happen on patrol. He stated that sometimes when the air was heavy and very still, the bushes on the grounds would rustle slightly, as if being gently prodded by an unseen force. It happened on rare occasions, but those on duty knew that it was a sign that something unusual was about to take place on one of the shifts. The ranger continued saying that sightings or "unexplained happenings" would inevitably be reported by one of the rangers. No one could ever explain the "phantom breeze" that caused the shrubs to move on their own when all the surrounding trees were still or the peculiar events that always followed.

One of the uncommon events involved an Alamo ranger hearing the sound of a bell while patrolling the long barracks. It wasn't a church bell but more like a "tinkle" or, as one ranger put it, "something like the bell that jingled at the end of the movie *It's A Wonderful Life.*" Those who heard the sound were never able to trace its locations but, in time, accepted the sound as a kind of "all-clear" signal from beyond—as if an "angel were watching over them."

Psychics have been known to make their way into the chapel or wander the Alamo grounds and "attach themselves to the walls, so to speak," said one ranger. "You could always tell when a clairvoyant was visiting the Alamo" stated another ranger, "because of the way they went around holding onto the walls, pressing their palms up against the façade, or standing up against them and concentrating and trying to pick up the vibes of the place. And there were a lot of vibrations inside the chapel."

On another occasion, a ranger recalled a discussion he had one day with a psychic who introduced herself. She proceeded to tell him that she had just viewed three Mexican soldiers standing near gate six, which is located facing East Houston in front of the gift shop. According to the psychic, it was as if the soldiers were "waiting for orders"; they were there for a beat, then gone. The psychic continued by saying that once inside the Alamo grounds, she distinctly saw a man near the long barracks wearing frontier clothes and pointing toward his socks! This was the first time the guard ever recalled hearing about an apparition's socks. The guard said, "Usually people see the outfits and weapons, not the shoes or socks." He wasn't doubting what the woman saw, only that this particular sighting was a bit stranger than most. Why would a ghost point toward his socks? Perhaps they needed mending after all these years!

On another occasion, two tile layers who were working in the museum gift shop walked outside to take a short break. As they stepped out into the daylight, they were stunned to see a man dressed in a "funny-looking western outfit" pass right through a wall near gate two, which is central to the long wall fronting Bonham Street. At the moment they witnessed the bizarre event, an employee rushed over. She seemed very agitated and asked both men if they had just seen the "strange-looking gentleman walk through the wall!" The men said they had seen something, but they weren't quite sure what. The startled men returned to work inside the gift shop but had trouble concentrating on their assignments the rest of the day; the lingering memory of the ghostly encounter was still etched in their minds.

A similar situation occurred when several men were repairing gate five between the chapel and the long barracks. As they were welding, one of the men happened to look up for a second. What he saw made him shout to his coworkers. Everyone stopped to stare at a figure of a man approximately six feet tall and wearing a frontier outfit crossing the grounds directly in front of them. The man was holding an "old-fashioned rifle," as the workers later recalled, and had vanished right in front of them. After standing with mouths agape, they ran to look for the man, thinking that some kind of costume party or reenactment was going on. They found no special event, no man in buckskin, nothing! The ghostly frontiersman had faded in and faded out right before their eyes.

Another long barracks account concerned a metal door inside the barracks, which is supposed to be open all night; however, this isn't always the case. Even after Alamo rangers secure the long barracks for the evening, making sure the metal door inside remains open for security reasons, there have been a number of occasions when the door has been found shut. There is no way this could happen without someone physically closing it, and the baffled rangers are unable to understand how or why this door sometimes refuses to remain open. There is no air conditioning inside after hours, and the door is not unbalanced nor are any trespassers responsible given the tight security and the fact that once the outer doors are sealed, the alarm system is turned on. Still, there are occasions when the doors are opened or a ranger inspects the interior of the long barracks during a shift, and the door will have managed to shut itself—or be closed by invisible hands.

167

The long barracks looking west
Photograph by Robert Wlodarski

Guests at the Menger Hotel across the street and to the south of the Alamo have often reported sightings from their north-facing windows, which overlook the shrine. One guest was looking out of his window late one night to view the grounds before turning in. The guest claims to have seen a woman in white standing on the outside wall in a mournful pose. She then disappeared as he watched in stunned silence. He reported the incident as he checked out the next morning. A room with a view of ghosts was not his idea of a relaxing vacation.

On another occasion, two guests were about to go to sleep. Before calling it a night, they decided to have another look at the Alamo from their fifth-floor window. When they parted the curtains, they were astonished to witness several campfires on the Alamo grounds with Native Americans parading around. They gazed at the unusual scene for a few minutes, not sure what was happening. They both concluded that it must be some sort of reenactment taking place because they heard that, on occasion, this did take place at the Alamo. Closing the curtains, thinking they had simply seen some kind of staged event, they retired for the night.

The next morning, they asked a bellboy about the "reenactment" and when it was going to start again. They explained what they witnessed the night before. The bellboy stopped, shook his head, and said that to his knowledge, there was no reenactment scheduled anytime soon, and even if there were, he was sure that no Native American scenes were ever portrayed. The confused couple decided to go to the Alamo personnel. They obtained the same answer—there was no reenactment the previous night and nothing taking place that day or in the near future. Perhaps the couple witnessed a scene from a time prior to the construction of the mission when Native Americans would have been present.

Another Menger-Alamo event took place after midnight involving two employees who were working in the area where guests check in with their cars and luggage. It was a relatively quiet summer night, humid, and without a breath of air. The two employees were passing time talking sports when something caught one employee's attention. Out of the corner of his eye, he saw soldiers passing by. He nudged his friend, and they both watched in silence as a group of six Mexican soldiers passed in front of them along East Crockett Street. As the last soldier passed, the employees remarked to one another about how authentic the uniforms and rifles looked. Like the aforementioned guests, the employees thought that it was some kind of reenactment or ceremony to honor the battle. Just to verify what they saw, both employees rushed out from behind their booth and looked down the street in the direction they last viewed the "soldiers." It had only been a few seconds, but as they gazed toward Alamo Plaza fully expecting to see the contingent, they were greeted instead by an empty street and total silence. Where had they disappeared so quickly? A quick search of Alamo Plaza and South Alamo revealed nothing. The flabbergasted employees returned to work with no explanation. After spending the rest of their shift discussing the incident, they were convinced that they had experienced a close encounter with the spirits of the Alamo.

The long barracks was also the scene of another terrifying incident involving an Alamo ranger. The ranger prefaced his story by stating that although he did not believe in the supernatural, many things that he could not explain had happened to him during his stint. He also said it was common knowledge among the rangers (though he said most wouldn't talk about it) that the long barracks were the focal point for strange encounters and that "unusual things" would happen inside all the time, including strange sounds, voices, and footsteps. On this particular occasion, the ranger was making his rounds, locking up after all the visitors were gone for the day. He walked through the long barracks as usual making sure that there weren't any stragglers. He stopped short. Before him was a gruesome scene. He stated, "It wasn't like seeing a ghost; it was as if I were talking to you." A defender stood against the wall with two bullet holes in his chest, bleeding profusely. The next second, two Mexican soldiers appeared with bayonets and began stabbing the poor defender over and over. Within ten seconds, the entire event played out and disappeared, leaving the ranger stunned and alone. After the ghastly scene dematerialized, the ranger quickly ran through the lock-up procedure, his hair standing on end the entire time. He didn't go back into the barracks the rest of the night. He insisted that he wasn't frightened, but the ranger clearly wanted no more "instant replays!"

Another ranger told of some classic encounters that have been experienced by various rangers, saying that he thought something unusual was going on inside the Alamo grounds late at night; however, he wouldn't go so far as to say it was "haunted." The most frequently related stories among rangers are those associated with voices and footsteps in the long barracks, vanishing frontier-clad men walking the Alamo grounds, strange cold spots, eerie sensations and noises within the chapel, a mysterious light above the chapel that appears then disappears, and the face of a boy in the high window of the gift shop. The ranger also said there were plenty of other lesser stories of brief visions, unearthly footsteps, discarnated voices, vanishing lights, and unexplained noises that cannot be accounted for. It is clear that the inexplicable phenomena are part of the long and memorable Alamo history, which continues to replay itself in time.

A Psychic Tunes in to the Alamo Tragedy

Surveys have shown that more than ten percent of the population claim they have seen ghosts. But what have they really seen: dead people coming back to life, images from their own minds, perhaps something like videotapes of reality played not at the wrong speed but at the wrong time? For most of us, time flows inexorably past like an escalator or a moving walkway in an airport. We get swept along, and we can't help getting older even if we never get much wiser! But, just occasionally, some people seem to stumble on images from another time. They somehow break the rules, and then they may see fragments from the future or glimpses of the past.

John Beckett, *World's Weirdest "True" Ghost Stories* (1991)

The authors of this book were fortunate enough to participate in a very special walk-through of the Alamo grounds with internationally known lecturer, author, and psychic consultant Kathleen Bittner and her husband, Dr. Hans Roth. This interview turned out to be very special in terms of content and emotion. Time passed so quickly that what took three hours to complete could have easily lasted three days, and we would have still only touched the tip of a paranormal iceberg of information. We saved this interview for the last part of our book, but we hope it is only the beginning of future investigations.

The interview with Bittner began inside the chapel; however, it quickly became too crowded with a group of tourists, so we moved outside to the front of the long barracks. Bittner soon began to receive psychic impressions and images of the day of the battle. She stated that what she sensed was not fear or panic in the people involved but rather a "feeling of bewilderment." This feeling may have come from the fact that conflicting orders were being given, especially because Travis died so quickly (he was one of the first casualties). Apparently, his death led to a breakdown in the direct line of command and part of the confusion that followed. The Alamo was being overrun, and since Bowie was unable to lead and lay close to death inside one of the buildings, Crockett was probably in charge.

For the men who had accepted Travis's command, losing their leader so quickly must have proved devastating. The loss of Travis combined with a four-sided attack and the fact that Crockett was trying to be everywhere at once issuing commands, most certainly contributed to the futility of the situation and feelings of bewilderment. One rarely finds more traumatic circumstances than where the odds are so lopsided and where a stable authoritative figure is missing—hence, the confusion.

Bittner also picked up on several changes made at the last minute in the placement and direction of the artillery, which did not correspond with the final direction of the onslaught. In a time of confusion, perhaps those remaining in charge were attempting to determine where the brunt of Santa Anna's forces would break through; therefore they were forced to scatter their energies during the final assault.

In hindsight, little could have been done to change the course of the battle unless the defenders could have assassinated Santa Anna or could have had a great deal more sharpshooters at their disposal. If conflicting orders had

173

been given as far as the placement of men or direction of artillery fire, the final outcome might have been prolonged, but the results would have been the same—total annihilation for the defenders. Perhaps the "feeling of tremendous bewilderment" surfaced from the fact that up until the time of the final assault, the men were still expecting reinforcements to come to their aid. When they realized that help was not forthcoming, feelings of abandonment, betrayal, confrontation with their own mortality, combined with their loss of leadership early in the battle created a kind of confusion that lasted beyond death—not only for the defenders but for the Mexican soldiers as well.

Amid such confusion, heroism, and sacrifice, the fact remains that many men on both sides gave their lives that day without fully comprehending the historical ramifications. They died brutally, unprepared for the horror and trauma of the event, with most not receiving a Christian burial after having given their lives for one cause or another. The psychic imprint of that day etched on the Alamo landscape appears as fresh today as on March 6, 1836.

Bittner next picked up on a woman and two small children inside the chapel. They were watching the battle from a small opening in the window. Bittner said that the woman she saw also had a bewildered look rather than one of fear as one might think. This re-emphasizes the point that what was taking place in the minds of the men, women, and children was uncertainty and confusion during the final stand. Only when everyone realized that no help was coming and that the chain of command was disintegrating did the situation become overwhelming. Before them lay only one certainty—they were going to die without mercy.

A strange feeling overtook all of us when we were inside the barracks. While walking past all of the display cases and photographs and upon entering each room, we saw a number of tourists milling around and talking. As Bittner picked up information on each of the men in the photographs, an eerie hush fell over the room. It was as if time stood still. Each time Bittner spoke, there was not even a whisper from those browsing in the room with us. We all had the "chills" as we noticed this phenomenon occurring. It wasn't as if the others were listening to our conversation, it was as if they were suspended in time or operating on a different frequency or level. Once Bittner stopped talking, it was as if a button had been pushed and everyone else became animated once again. This happened on two occasions while passing from south to north through the barracks. On many occasions, we all broke out in goose bumps, particularly when discussing the battle. Additionally, we sensed being watched or somebody brushing by, as if invisible people were near—listening.

Bittner also sensed that someone may have been providing Santa Anna with detailed information as to the defenders' strengths and weaknesses. Perhaps it was an informant who may have appeared neutral to the defenders and was able to slip in and out of the compound to deliver updates. Bittner did not come up with a name, only a very strong feeling that throughout the siege, messages were being delivered to Santa Anna with regard to gun positions or other tactical data. The trusting men inside were never aware that their position was being compromised. We do know that to the very end, messengers rode to and from the Alamo. It is also believed that for a time, Bowie and Travis were attempting to communicate with Santa Anna. The fact that someone inside could have been a spy for Santa Anna is a possibility even though it has not been substantiated. (It is a fact that the "Yellow Rose of Texas," Emily Morgan, was a spy for the Texians prior to the battle of San Jacinto.)

175

Bittner also sensed that there was a priest who visited the Alamo before the battle to minister to the needs of any Catholics, and perhaps afterwards to administer last rights to the fallen soldiers. This priest might have been able to pass information back and forth. Research indicates that although there was no priest residing at the Alamo, the civilian community was probably served by the local priest at the San Fernando Mission, who at that time was Father Refugio De La Garza.

As Bittner passed the photograph of Juan Nepomuceno Seguin, only twenty-nine years old at the time of the battle, she felt that his spirit remains because of "unfinished business." She sensed that he is not at peace and remains behind to right a wrong. For twenty-nine-year-old James Butler Bonham of Edgefield County, South Carolina, this lifetime was a "rite of passage." Bittner felt that Bonham's sacrifice was extremely tragic in the sense that he never was able to marry and have children; something he desired and regarded highly. Unfulfilled love and sacrifice were to be his destiny.

For William Barret Travis, a twenty-six-year-old lawyer, newspaperman, and teacher from Red Banks Church in South Carolina, the energy surrounding him was not easily discernable. Travis was an enigmatic man, and the whole story regarding his actions at the Alamo has yet to be told. This was a man who left his home and family after his wife had an affair with a riverboat gambler. Travis was then charged with murder and fled to Texas. He left behind a pregnant wife who bore him a daughter, Susan Isabella, three months after his departure from South Carolina. Travis gave his hammered gold ring set with black cat's eye to Angelina Dickinson, possibly thinking of his own daughter whom he had never seen.

With forty-nine-year-old David Crockett of Green County, Tennessee, Bittner immediately sensed a dedicated and loyal man who was committed to a cause he was willing to die for. As Bittner stood in front of Crockett's portrait and put her hands up to the protective case, a strong smell of resin or gunpowder filtered through the area where we stood; within seconds, the smell dissipated.

Bittner paused for a few moments in front of James Walker Fannin's portrait and picked up on a very strong, peaceful, and attentive spirit—that of a man who has not been honored as he should but blamed instead for not coming to the aid of the Alamo defenders. Bittner felt that this type of accusation was unjustified given that Fannin had received conflicting orders and encountered so many problems while attempting to leave Goliad to reach the Alamo.

Standing in back of the long barracks, Bittner reaffirmed that this area was a tremendously intense energy spot where so much had happened to a great many men quite suddenly; the impression of that moment is indelibly etched in time.

Men from both sides were caught in a deadly barrage of artillery fire. They were also locked in hand-to-hand combat, fighting to the death—chaos was everywhere. According to Bittner, the psychic imprints of the carnage that occurred in the long barracks and near the chapel is still "fresh and very painful."

After leaving the long barracks, Bittner summarized her impressions by stating that the energies surrounding the barracks, chapel, defenders, women and children, and the Mexican soldiers all reflect an overall feeling of confusion and betrayal rather than fear or anger. She felt very strongly that there is tremendous energy surrounding the Alamo as if these spirits are wandering about looking for answers.

The energies that remain are locked in the same state of consciousness. These are souls who wander throughout the Alamo grounds, passing in and out of the walls all of the time, seeking freedom from their state of confusion and trauma—they seemed "stunned." Bittner felt that the energies of the Mexican soldiers were wandering aimlessly near the south end of the long barracks while the strongest "defender" energy was near the north end.

Standing in the area where the cattle pen was located behind the long barracks, Bittner sensed a young boy trapped in time. She picked up the name Thomas (or Tomas in Spanish). She indicated that the boy peeps down from a window in the gift shop (mentioned by former Alamo ranger W.M. earlier in the book). Bittner sensed that the boy would have been somewhere in the area, responsible for watching the livestock. He was small for his age, maybe ten or eleven years old, and felt a great deal of accountability for the defeat—that he could have done more to prevent the slaughter. Bittner said that children often take on more than their share of guilt.

The boy's spirit remains behind as if seeking an affirmation that he did a good job while alive—a task for which he was never rewarded. He was separated from the others when a breakthrough occurred during the battle that involved the livestock area. Bittner felt that he hovers about, asking those who pass by for forgiveness. The poor soul sees all those who come and go and asks them for assurance that he did nothing wrong.

Bittner also remarked that as she passed through the chapel, there were definitely energies inside. She confirmed that upon entering the chapel, to the immediate right, she saw a vision of a "woman and two children huddled in the corner." The child on her left was taller and about eleven years of age while the one on her right was approximately six years old and smaller. She said that the feminine energy is strong inside the chapel and accounts for much of the lingering energy, shadows, and voices remaining behind.

Moving to the acequia, Bittner picked up on "fresh blood" in this area where there was an intense struggle and great loss of life—carnage was one word that repeatedly came to her while in this location.

As with any historical account, there are so many perspectives, that the "truth" is extremely subjective. What really happened to these men during the final assault when they knew there was no hope for survival is speculation. If "bewilderment," as Bittner repeated again and again, was the strongest emotion she sensed, this would lead one to speculate about what the men were being told. Were the defenders still being assured until the bitter end that help was on the way, even though all hope had long since passed?

Were the estimates of the forces against them being understated? Were the men being told that negotiations for peace were still ongoing prior to the final onslaught? It seems that only the restless, wandering spirits of the Alamo know the answers to the questions and the ultimate truths as to what really happened in the final moments of the battle.

Other Haunted Hot Spots Near the Alamo

Some believe that ghosts are merely figments of the imagination, illusions based on unfounded superstitions, hallucinations, or dreams and nightmares that only seem real. Possibly, what are thought to be hauntings are merely the residue of intense emotions, feelings, or something experienced by someone on a particular spot or in a specific place many years before. My dilemma is that I find it just as difficult to believe in ghosts as I find it difficult to disbelieve in them. The question of ghosts has, of course, perplexed living souls since shortly after Adam and Eve, and we seem no closer to an answer now than we did then.

Robert Ellis Cahill, *Haunted Happenings* (1992)

Because the battle of the Alamo encompassed such a large area, with the final assault coming essentially from all directions, and given the tremendous loss of life and intensity of the fighting through the final days of late February and early March 1836, it is no wonder that paranormal activity extends to a number of buildings that lie within a few blocks of the Alamo. It was all one large, bloody battlefield where many men died. Additionally, the Alamo and surrounding area were used as a mission prior to the 1836 battle and witnessed battles involving Native Americans as well as the deaths of many Spaniards, neophyte laborers, and early settlers, many of whom are buried in front of the Alamo and within the walls of the chapel. What better place to encounter the paranormal!

With this in mind, the following places, which lie within the original Alamo battlefield, have their own other-worldly tales to tell. Some stories relate to the early history of the Alamo and to the actual battle while other accounts pertain to events that occurred within the particular establishment. They have no bearing on the history of the Alamo other than the fact that the establishment happens to be situated within the area where many people lost their lives in a very traumatic way. For additional information regarding specifics of nearby locations with a haunted past, please refer to *Spirits of San Antonio and South Texas* by Williams and Byrne (1993). Although the following locations are open to the public, make every effort to be courteous and considerate when visiting these haunted establishments.

See for yourself if you are able to sense something while spending the night or just walking through—you can be sure that as you are looking for discarnate energy or apparitions, they are probably watching you as well and deciding whether or not to make themselves known. If your hair suddenly stands on end or you feel cold whips of air pass by you, then there is a good chance you are partaking in a paranormal encounter! A map has been provided that illustrates the battle area in relation to the Alamo (A) and various reported haunted locales.

B—The Menger Hotel—Located across the street from the Alamo at 204 Alamo Plaza. According to publicity information, the Menger Hotel dates to 1859 when it became the first major hotel in San Antonio. The majestic front offers a unique view of Alamo Plaza. The older portion of the hotel overlooks the courtyard and tropical garden. The newer rooms of the hotel face the Alamo, which, at night, offer a spectacular view of the historic chapel. The Menger is host to a number of recorded phenomena, including several spirits who are known to

Other Haunted Hot Spots Near the Alamo

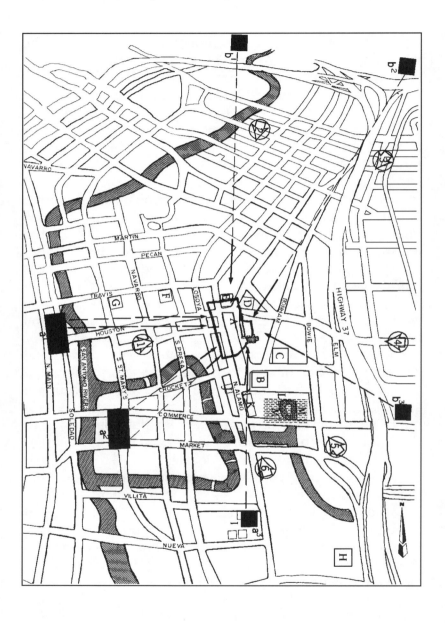

The 1836 Battle of the Alamo in Relation to Modern Landmarks
(Including Buildings Which are Reputed to be Haunted)

Legend

A	The Alamo Complex	G	Gunter Hotel
B	Menger Hotel	H	Institute of Texan Cultures
C	Crockett Hotel	I	La Villita
D	Ramada Emily Morgan Hotel	J	Booksmith's
E	U.S. Post Office	K	Dillards
F	Crowne Plaza St. Anthony Hotel	L	Rivercenter Mall
M	Possible Location of Funeral Pyre		
a	Probable Mexican Artillery Locations	b	Probable Direction of Mexican
a1	Near Soledad & Houston Streets		Artillery Fire
a2	Near S. St. Mary's & Commerce Streets	b1	Near Dallas & Albany Streets
a3	Near Cos House (Presa Street/La Villita)	b2	Near Walnut & Sherry Streets
		b3	Near N. Pine & N. Olive Streets

1   Attack from General Cos (Aldama Battalion and 3 Cos. San Luis Potosi - Mexican Infantry) - First attack reached the west wall and was repulsed. The battalion swung north to join Colonel Duque's Toluca Infantry Battalion and were again forced back. The third charge was successful and the remainder of the infantry scaled the walls and opened the gate near the northwest corner of the Quadrangle.

2   Colonel Duque (Toluca Battalion and 3 Cos. San Luis Potosi - Mexican Infantry) - Attacked the north walls of the Quadrangle and were twice repulsed. The third attack broke through the walls and entered the Quadrangle with Cos's Battalion.

3   Colonel Amat (Zapadores Battalion and Grenadiers - Mexican Reserves) - Joined the final assault of the Alamo along the north wall of the Quadrangle with the other commanders.

4   Colonel Romero (Jimenez Battalion and 2 Cos. Matamoros Fusiliers - Mexican Infantry) - Attacked the south wall of the Convent Courtyard, was stopped short of the wall, then veered north toward the northeast wall of the Quadrangle where his attacked stalled. Finally on the third attempt, his Battalion broke through along with Colonel Duque and Colonel Amat's forces.

5   The Dolores Dragoons (Mexican Cavalry) - Guard the southern portion of the Alamo near the Chapel and Palisade area.

6   Colonel Morales (Chasseurs - Mexican Infantry) - Attack the Palisade area defended by Crockett's Volunteers. They are repulsed by deadly fire and move along the Low Barrack to find shelter. On the final assault, they overrun the battery near the southwest corner of the Quadrangle.

Adapted from (Historic Sites - San Antonio, Alamo Map file, **DRT Library**; Unique Map of the ALAMO Battlefield, **San Antonio Express News**, 3/6/1995; Fall of the Alamo map, by Parker's Press (1988); and Map of San Antonio, **You Are Here Company** (1994).

183

frequent the Menger Bar late at night, and the fourth floor in the older section of the hotel where the ghost of Sallie White has been occasionally spotted. There are also reports of those who have slept in rooms facing the Alamo seeing ghostly soldiers walking the Alamo grounds, then vanishing; unexplainable campfires and guards on the walls appear and disappear as startled guests look on.

C—The Best Western Crockett Hotel—Located at 320 Bonham (at Crockett Street in back of the Alamo). The Crockett was built in 1909 and has been completely restored. The hotel is a historic Texas landmark with 202 spacious and beautifully decorated guest rooms with ghostly activities centering in the lobby where the entrance doors will occasionally open and close without being triggered by a human being; the bar area, and certain rooms in the hotel where faint whispers, colds spots, and a variety of unexplainable activities have taken place over the years.

D—The Ramada Emily Morgan Hotel—Located across the street and north of the Alamo at the intersection of 705 East Houston Street and Avenue E. It is a relatively new hotel that was once the Medical Arts Building. It was constructed in 1924 by J.M. Nix, who later built the Nix Hospital and Majestic Theater in San Antonio. Sightings have occurred on the seventh floor and in the lobby where ghostly manifestations, cold spots, and mysterious noises have occurred. The basement used to be the morgue when the structure was used as a Medical Arts Building. The hotel is named after the Yellow Rose of Texas, Emily (Wells) Morgan, who, according to legend, was partially responsible for Santa Anna's delayed response to the Texas charge on April 21, 1836, at San Jacinto.

E—The U.S. Post Office—Located near the corner of North Alamo, E. Houston Street and Avenue E. Based on information provided from security personnel, several employees have witnessed paranormal activity. Discarnate voices, doors slamming shut on their own, lights turning on and off, and other phenomena in the basement, lobby, and fifth floor over the years have been substantiated. A recent sighting involved a guard who watched in disbelief as a middle-aged couple walked toward him on the fifth floor and vanished right in front of him.

F—The Crowne Plaza St. Anthony Hotel—Located at 300 E. Travis at Navarro. The St. Anthony with its rich heritage has been designated a Texas and National Historic Landmark. Named after the city and saint (San Antonio de Padua), the hotel was constructed in 1909 by B.L. Naylor and A.H. Jones (Jones was the mayor of San Antonio from 1912-1913). A renovation in recent years has restored the 1909 hotel to its prior state of elegance with oriental rugs, antiques, and chandeliers gracing the lobby and other areas. The "spiritual" side of the hotel boasts many ghostly apparitions. On the roof (which used to host many of the nation's top big bands from the 1920s through 1941) children and a woman in a ball gown have been frequently sighted. It is considered a "hot bed" of paranormal activity. Other strange sightings have been reported along a fourth-floor corridor, the men's locker area in the basement, a kitchen corridor that is haunted by a ghostly woman, and various rooms throughout the hotel. Allegedly, a mysterious event and unsolved murder at the nearby Gunter Hotel ended in tragedy for the man accused of the murder in room 536 at the St. Anthony. Staff has reported seeing a woman in ghostly attire as well as an elderly woman in a long, white gown in the room (see Williams and Byrne 1993:53-59).

G—The Sheraton Gunter Hotel—Located at 205 E. Houston at St. Mary's Street. The history of the Gunter Hotel began in 1837 when the Frontier Inn was built on the site of the present-day hotel. In 1851 the site became

185

the United States Military Headquarters; from 1861 to 1865 it served as Confederate headquarters; in 1872, as the Vance House; and in 1886 was renamed the Mahncke Hotel. In 1909 the *San Antonio Express* declared, "Out of the ruins of the Mahncke Hotel will rise a palatial structure." The Gunter Hotel became reality because of real estate developer L.J. Hart and twelve local investors including Jot Gunter, who purchased the site from Mary E. Vance Winslow in 1907. The 301 room, eight-story building was the largest hotel in San Antonio at the time and became the center of social life. With its fame and notoriety came the inevitable stories of hauntings. Room 636 (now changed to another number) became legendary as being the spot of one of San Antonio's greatest unsolved mysteries which tragically concluded at the St. Anthony Hotel in room 536—the "murder room" at the Gunter, which is reportedly haunted. The ballroom is another area where repeated unexplainable occurrences have taken place and psychic activity is strong. Photographs of employees and guests have been developed at a variety of functions showing guests from another time appearing as unidentifiable transparent guests partying alongside the living. There have also been a number of peculiar disturbances reported in the elevators, and phantom voices and mysterious shadows appearing on corridor walls have been reported by guests and employees near room 426. A man named Buck, a long-term tenant who died in the hotel, is still seen wandering near his room, and the Lady in Blue are but a few of the many Gunter ghostly guests.

H—The Institute of Texan Cultures—Located in HemisFair Park at Bowie and Durango Streets. The history of Texas and its varied ethnic background is highlighted in the many exhibits on display at the Institute. The library houses important photographic and documentary information for researchers no matter where their particular interests in Texas history lie. The ITC also houses a few apparitions on the second floor as well as near the loading dock in the back of the building. It is here that a kindly man is said to have returned to bid adieu to the place he worked. As the man lay on his deathbed in another part of town, an employee spotted him performing his duties. He called out to the man who smiled and walked away. The employee told his supervisor that he had seen the elderly man even though he wasn't supposed to be at work that day. What made the situation even more strange was the fact that the man was wearing non-working attire, which the employee also took note of. The supervisor's mouth dropped open since word had arrived that the man had just passed away. They later found out that the man had requested the next of kin to bury him in the exact outfit described by the employee, the day of the encounter. Perhaps it was a final farewell to a job he loved.

I—La Villita—Bounded by Nueva, South Alamo, South Presa Streets, and the San Antonio River, La Villita has been restored and now looks more like it did originally. From San Antonio's historic beginnings, there has been a settlement in La Villita. General Cos surrendered to the Texians at a house that still stands on Villita Street. Although La Villita is associated primarily with the Mexican population of San Antonio, it has since become the home of many artisan shops, small businesses, and a few ghosts. The Cos House, 504 Villita Street has been a school, apartment building, art gallery, and lapidary shop; the Starving Artists Gallery was once the Warren Hunter Art School; and Dasheill House at 511 Paseo La Villita Street was built in 1849-1850. One of the focal points for artillery fire during the battle of the Alamo, La Villita appears to continue keeping the spirit of the 1836 battle alive.

J—Booksmiths—The store is located at 209 Alamo Plaza at Crockett Street. Booksmiths lies within the original battlefield grounds southwest of the Alamo. The store carries a wonderful collection of books dealing with Texas history and also appears to serve as a library for its ghostly inhabitants. Employees report finding items in the store moved around when they open in the morning. Equipped with an alarm system, no one enters after the door is secured yet, somehow, books and items on shelves that require a ladder to reach are found on the floor, far away from where they were placed the night before.

K—Dillard's—Located on North Alamo next to the Menger Hotel. It was originally called Joske's and opened in 1875 on Alamo Plaza as Joske Brothers. In 1888 the store moved again to its present location on Commerce and Alamo. The two-story department store was famous for "The Big Sign" that loomed over Alamo Plaza for a number of years. In 1987 Joske's closed for remodeling while the Rivercenter Mall was being built on an old parking lot. It never reopened as Joske's but became Dillard's. Rumors persist that apparitions roam both levels of the department store after hours. Several incidents have been reported involving phantom voices, items moving on their own, and disembodied spirits floating across the aisles. The haunting activity is relatively quiet by day, the spirits perhaps preferring to shop for bargains after hours!

L & M—The Rivercenter Mall—The mall is located at Commerce and Bowie Streets. The regional shopping center built during 1987 is a massive architectural achievement with the river diverted through the sprawling mall. Some historians claim that the mall was constructed over the site of the funeral pyre where the remains of the Alamo defenders were carried to be burned. It may also have been the spot where the bodies of many Mexican soldiers were unceremoniously dumped due to lack of burial space in a local cemetery. There are rumors of unexplainable late night noises and apparitions, which appear in various portions of the mall. Security guards were reluctant to discuss the topic of ghosts although they did not deny that strange things have taken place over the years. This is understandable considering that the mall may sit on top of an area where hundreds of bodies may have been cremated, dumped into the river, or buried.

As a final thought, no one who has seen, heard, or felt something while at the Alamo to date has ever expressed a feeling of being threatened or sensed that they would be harmed in any way. People have stated over and over that a healthy fear of the unknown has been present in most who have had an encounter, but this is a natural emotion. In fact, the overall impression from those who have been fortunate enough to have partaken in the paranormal phenomena is that it left them exhilarated and refreshed and that it was exciting and even fun. As one person stated after an encounter, "They are just doing their thing while we do ours." If we do happen to enter their world, we should just say "excuse me" and move on.

The Alamo has its share of the paranormal because it represents a time and place where ideals meant everything. Those who gave up their lives did so because they believed in a cause; however, most died in the prime of their lives and under extreme and tragic circumstances. The nature of the battle and the fact that the end came swiftly and violently for most represents classic conditions for a haunting. Therefore, the Alamo represents an ongoing case study of the paranormal in the same vein as Gettysburg. Battlefields, in particular, are areas where tourists, rangers, psychics, and the dead co-exist as they attempt to find a common ground to communicate and hopefully resolve issues which keep the dead "alive" in this dimension.

We hope you enjoy your visit to the Alamo and San Antonio. Good luck and . . .

Happy Haunting!

Useful Names and Numbers

The Alamo Visitors Center—(210) 225-8587

The Alamo—300 Alamo Plaza, P.O. Box 2599, San Antonio, Texas 78299—(210) 255-1391

Alamodome—I-37 at Market Street—(210) 207-3663

Brackenridge Park—3800 Broadway—(210) 821-3000

Daughters of the Republic of Texas Library—P.O. Box 1401, San Antonio, Texas 78295-1401—(210) 225-1071

Hauntings History of San Antonio—Ghost tours conducted by Martin Leal every day of the year—(210) 436-5417

Hemisfair Park—(210) 299-8572

IMAX Theater—(210) 225-4629

Institute of Texan Cultures—HemisFair Park—(210) 226-7651

Instituto Cultural Mexicano—600 HemisFair Park—(210) 227-0123

Japanese Tea Gardens—3800 N. St. Mary's Street—(210) 821-3000

King William Historic District—King William Street and surrounding area

La Villita—(210) 299-8610

The Navarro House—228 South Laredo at Nueva Street—(210) 226-4801

San Antonio Chamber of Commerce—602 E. Commerce at Alamo St.—(210) 229-2100

San Antonio Conservation Society—Anton Wulff House, 107 King William—(210) 224-6163

San Antonio Convention and Visitors Bureau—121
Alamo Plaza at Commerce—(210) 270-8700

San Antonio River Association (PASEO DEL RIO
ASSOCIATION)—213 Broadway at Travis—(210)
227-4262

The *San Antonio Express-News*—Avenue E and Third
Street—(210) 225-7144

San Fernando Cathedral—114 Main Street—(210)
227-1297

Sea World—10500 Sea World Drive—(210) 523-3611

Spanish Governors' Palace—105 Military Plaza—(210)
224-0601

Visitor Information Center—317 Alamo Plaza at
Houston—(210) 299-8155

Yturri-Edmunds House and Mill—257 Yellowstone—
(210) 534-8237

Reference Material

Alexander, John. *Ghosts: Washington's Most Famous Ghost Stories*. The Washington Book Trading Company, Virginia, 1988.

Auerback, Loyd. *ESP, Hauntings and Poltergeists*. Warner Books, Inc. N.Y., 1986.

Bayless, Raymond. *The Enigma of the Poltergeist*. Parker Publishing Co., West Nyack, N.Y., 1967.

_____*Apparitions and Survival of Death*. University Books, New Hyde Park, N.Y., 1973.

Beckett, John.*World's Weirdest "True" Ghost Stories*. Sterling Publishing Co., Inc. New York, 1991.

Boyd, Bob. *The Texas Revolution: A Day-by-Day Account*. Kevin Barry Publisher, Standard-Times, San Angelo, Texas, 1986.

Bingham, Joan, and Dolores Riccio. *More Haunted Houses*. Pocket Books, N.Y., 1991.

Cahill, Robert Ellis. *New England's Ghostly Haunts*. Chandler-Smith Publishing House, Inc., 1983.

_____*Haunted Happenings*. Old Saltbox Publishing House, Inc., Salem, Massachusetts, 1992.

Carrico, Richard L. *San Diego's Spirits: Ghosts and Hauntings in America's Southwest Corner*. Recuerdos Press, San Diego, 1991.

Chariton, Wallace O., Charlie Eckhardt and Kevin R. Young. *Unsolved Texas Mysteries*. Wordware Publishing, Inc., Plano, Texas, 1991.

Cohen, Daniel. *Real Ghosts*. Pocket Books, New York, 1977.

_____*The Encyclopedia of Ghosts*. Dodd, Mead and Co., N.Y., 1984.

Coleman, Loren. *Mysterious America*. Faber & Faber, Winchester, Mass., 1983.

_____*Curious Encounters*. Faber & Faber, Winchester, Mass., 1985.

Daughters of the Republic of Texas. *The Alamo Long Barrack Museum*. Alamo Museum Gift Shop, San Antonio, Texas, 1986.

DeBolt, Margaret Wayt. *Savannah Specters and Other Strange Tales*. The Donning Company Publishers, Norfolf, Virginia Beach, 1984.

Eaton, Jack. *Excavations at the Alamo Shrine (Mission San Antonio De Valero)*. Center for Archaeological Research, The University of Texas at San Antonio, Special Report No. 10, San Antonio, 1980.

Eysenck, Hans J., and Carl Sargent. *Explaining the Unexplained: Mysteries of the Paranormal*. Weidenfeld and Nicolson, London, 1982.

Fehrenbach, T.R. *Lone Star: A History of Texas and the Texans*. American Legacy Press, New York, 1968.

Forman, Joan. *The Haunted South*. Jarrold Publications, Norwich, Great Britain, 1978.

Foster, Nancy Haston and Benjamin A. Fairbank. *San Antonio*. Gulf Publishing Company, Houston, Texas, 1994.

Fox, Anne. *Archaeological Investigations In Alamo Plaza, San Antonio, Bexar County, Texas*. Center for Archaeological Research, The University of Texas at San Antonio, Archaeological Survey Report, No. 25, San Antonio, 1992.

Fox, Anne, Feris A. Bass Jr., and Thomas Hester. *The Archaeology and History of Alamo Plaza*. Center for

Archaeological Research, The University of Texas at San Antonio, Archaeological Survey Report, No. 16, San Antonio, 1976.

Groneman, Bill. *Alamo Defenders*. Eakin Press, Austin, Texas, 1990.

Guerra, Mary Ann Noonan. *The Alamo*. The Alamo Press, 1996.

Hard, Robert (Editor). *A Historical Overview of Alamo Plaza and Camposanto*. Center for Archaeological Research, The University of Texas at San Antonio, Special Report, No. 20, San Antonio, 1994.

Holzer, Hans. *Ghosts of the Golden West*. The Bobbs-Merrill Co., N.Y./also Ace Books, 1968.

_____*Haunted Hollywood*. The Bobbs-Merrill Co., N.Y., 1974.

_____*True Ghost Stories*. Prentice Hall, Englewood Cliffs, N.J., 1983.

_____*Where The Ghosts Are: The Ultimate Guide to Haunted Houses*. A Citadel Press Book, New York, 1995.

Inglis, Brian. *The Paranormal: An Encyclopedia of Psychic Phenomena*. Granada Publishing, London, 1985.

Jacobson, Laurie, and Marc Wanamaker. *Hollywood Haunted. A Ghostly Tour of Filmland*. Angel City Press, Santa Monica, 1994.

Jarvis, Sharon. *True Tales of the Unknown*. Bantam Books, N.Y., 1985.

_____*Dead Zones*. Warner Books, Inc., N.Y., 1992.

Keel, John. *Our Haunted Planet*. Fawcett Gold Medal Books, Greenwich, Conn., 1971.

King, C. Richard. *Susanna Dickinson: Messenger of the Alamo*. Shoal Creek Publishers, Inc. Austin, Texas, 1976.

Lord, Walter. *A Time to Stand: The Epic of the Alamo*. University of Nebraska Press, Lincoln, 1961.

MacKenzie, Andrew. *The Unexplained: Some Strange Cases of Psychical Research*. Popular Library, N.Y., 1970.

_____*Hauntings and Apparitions*. Granada Publishing, London, 1982.

Marinacci, Mike. *Mysterious California*. Panpipes Press, Los Angeles, 1988.

May, Antoinette. *Haunted Houses and Wandering Ghosts of California*. Examiner Special Projects, San Francisco, 1977.

_____*Haunted Houses of California*. Wide World Publishing/Tetra, San Carlos, CA., 1993.

McNeil, W.K. *Ghost Stories from the American South*. August House, Little Rock, Arkansas, 1985.

Martin, Maryjoy. *Twilight Dwellers: The Ghosts, Ghouls and Goblins of Colorado*. Pruett Publishing, Boulder, Colorado, 1985.

Mead, Robin. *Haunted Hotels*. Rutledge Hill Press, Nashville, Tennessee, 1995.

Matovina, Timothy M. *The Alamo Remembered: Tejano Accounts and Perspectives*. University of Texas Press, Austin, 1995.

Myers, Arthur. *The Ghostly Register.* Contemporary Books, Chicago, 1986.

_____*The Ghostly Gazetteer: America's Most Fascinating Haunted Landmarks*. Contemporary Books, Chicago, 1990.

Myers, John Myers. *The Alamo.* University of Nebraska Press, Lincoln, 1948.

Myers, L.F. *History, Battles and Fall of the Alamo.* Riverside Printing Company, Milwaukee, 1896.

Nesbitt, Mark. *More Ghosts of Gettysburg, Spirits, Apparitions and Haunted Places of the Battlefield.* Thomas Publications, Gettysburg, Pennsylvania, 1992.

Norman, Diana. *The Stately Ghosts of England.* Dorset Press, N.Y., 1977.

Oppel, Frank. *Tales of the New England Coast.* Castle, Secaucus, N.J., 1985.

Potter, R.M. *The Fall of the Alamo: A Reminiscence of the Revolution of Texas.* Reprinted by Fuller Printing Company, Bryan, Texas, 1979.

Randles, Jenny, and Peter Hough. *The Afterlife: An Investigation Into the Mysteries of Life After Death.* BerkleyBooks, N.Y., 1993.

Reinstedt, Randall. *Ghostly Tales and Mysterious Happennings of Old Monterey.* Ghost Town Publications, Carmel, California, 1977.

_____*Incredible Ghosts of Old Monterey's Hotel Del Monte.* Ghost Town Publications, Carmel, California, 1980.

Roberts, Nancy. *America's Most Haunted Places.* Sandlapper Publishing Company, Orangeburg, South Carolina, 1974.

_____*Haunted Houses.* The Globe Pequot Press, Old Saybrook, Connecticut, 1995.

Robinson, Charles Turek. *The New England Ghost Files, An Authentic Compendium of Frightening Phantoms.* Covered Bridge Press, Maryland, 1994.

Rogo, Scott D. *An Experience of Phantoms*. Taplinger, N.Y., 1974.

_____*Parapsychology: A Century of Inquiry*. Dutton, N.Y., 1977.

Ruth, Kent. *Landmarks of the West: A Guide to Historic Sites*. University of Nebraska Press, Lincoln, 1963.

Rybczyk, Mark Louis. *San Antonio Uncovered*. Wordware Publishing, Inc., Plano, Texas, 1992.

Scott, Beth, and Michael Norman. *Haunted Heartland*. Warner Books, N.Y., 1987.

_____*Haunted America*. A Tom Doherty Associates Book, New York, 1994.

_____*Historic Haunted America*. A Tom Doherty Associates Book, New York, 1995.

Senate, Richard L. *Ghosts of Southern California*. Pathfinder Publishing, Ventura, 1986.

_____*Ghosts of the Haunted Coast*. Pathfinder Publishing, Ventura, 1985.

_____*The Haunted Southland*. Charon Press, Ventura, California, 1994.

Smith, Susy. *Prominent American Ghosts*. The World Publishing Company, N.Y./ also Dell, N.Y., 1967.

_____*Haunted Houses for the Millions*. Bell Publishing Company, N.Y., 1967.

Steiger, Sherry Hansen, and Brad Steiger. *Hollywood and the Supernatural*. St. Martin's Press, N.Y., 1990.

Taylor, L.B., Jr. *The Ghosts of Virginia*. 248 Archer's Mead, Williamsburg, Virginia, 1993.

_____*The Ghosts of Virginia, Volume II*. 248 Archer's Mead, Williamsburg, Virginia, 1994.

USA Weekend. *Never Believed In Ghosts Until . . : 100 Real-Life Encounters*. Contemporary Books, Chicago, 1991.

Viviano, Christy L. *Haunted Louisiana*. Tree House Press, Metairie, Louisiana, 1992.

Warren, Ed and Lorraine, and Robert David Chase. *Ghost Hunters*. St. Martin's Paperbacks, N.Y., 1991.

_____*Graveyard: True Tales from and Old New England Cemetery*. St. Martin's Paperbacks, N.Y., 1992.

Webb, Richard. *Great Ghosts of the West*. Nash, Los Angeles, 1971.

Williams, Brad, and Choral Pepper. *The Mysterious West*. World Publishing, N.Y., 1967.

_____*Lost Legends of the West*. Holt, Rinehart & Winston, N.Y., 1970.

Williams, Docia Schultz. *Ghosts Along the Texas Coast*. Republic of Texas Press, Plano, Texas, 1995.

_____*Phantoms of the Plains: Tales of West Texas Ghosts*. Republic of Texas Press, Plano, Texas, 1996.

Williams, Docia Schultz, and Reneta Byrne. *Spirits of San Antonio and South Texas*. Republic of Texas Press, Plano, Texas, 1993.

Winer, Richard, and Nancy Osborn. *Haunted Houses*. Bantam Books, N.Y., 1979.

Wlodarski, Robert J., and Anne Nathan-Wlodarski. *Haunted Catalina: A History of the Island and Guide to Paranormal Activity*. G-Host Publishing, Calabasas, California, 1995.

Wlodarski, Robert J., Anne Powell Wlodarski, and Richard Senate. *A Guide to the Haunted Queen Mary: Ghostly Apparitions, Psychic Phenomena and Paranormal Activity*. G-Host Publishing,Calabasas, California, 1995.

Yeates, Geoff. *Cambridge College Ghosts*. Jarrold Publishing, Norwich, Great Britain, 1994.

Index

Other books from Republic of Texas Press

Alamo Movies

Alamo Story: From Early History to Current Conflicts

At Least 1836 Things You Ought to Know About Texas But Probably Don't

Battlefields of Texas

Best Tales of Texas Ghosts

Bubba Speak: Texas Folk Sayings

A Cowboy of the Pecos

Critter Chronicles

Dallas Uncovered (2nd Edition)

Daughter of Fortune: The Bettie Brown Story

Death of a Legend: The Myth & Mystery of Davy Crockett

Defense of a Legend

Dirty Dining

Etta Place: Her Life and Times with Butch Cassidy and the Sundance Kid

Exotic Pets: A Veterinary Guide for Owners

Exploring Branson: A Family Guide

Exploring Dallas with Children (2nd Edition)

Exploring New Orleans: A Family Guide

Exploring San Antonio with Children

Exploring Texas with Children

Exploring the Alamo Legends

Eyewitness to the Alamo

First in the Lone Star State

Fixin' to Be Texan

The Funny Side of Texas

Ghosts Along the Texas Coast

Ghosts of the Alamo

Good Times in Texas

The Great Texas Airship Mystery

Horses and Horse Sense

The King Ranch Story: Truth and Myth

The Last of the Old-Time Cowboys

Lawmen of the Old West

Letters Home: A Soldier's Legacy

Making it Easy: Cajun Cooking

Volunteers in the Texas Revolution: The New Orleans Greys

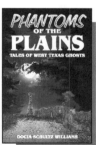

Phantoms of the Plains

Puncher Pie and Cowboy Lies

Rainy Days in Texas Funbook

Red River Women

Return of Assassin John Wilkes Booth

Other books from Republic of Texas Press

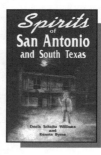
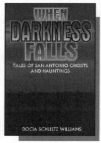